The Cann

by

M.L. Mirabello, Ph.D.

Published by

Mandrake of Oxford

PO Box 250

OXFORD

OX1 1AP (UK)

A CIP catalogue record for this book is available from the British Library and the US Library of Congress.

ISBN 1 86992827X

Author's Note

A Warning

I will now reveal the facts to you—the hard, inexorable, terrible facts. The truth is not beautiful—it stands on cloven hoofs—it is covered with coagulated blood—but it is the truth.

The human race does not control its own destiny. We may think we are free—millions of brainwashed simians living in a corn-fed Babylon called America believe this fantasy—but it is all an illusion. We are slaves—livestock—tethered on a long and invisible leash.

'The Earth is a farm,' wrote Charles Fort. 'We are someone else's property.'

We may think we are special—holy, honored, valued—god's chosen primates—but that is a fraud. The dupes of superhuman forces, we are misfits and abominations. We have no higher purpose—no savior god died for our sins—

we exist, only because our masters are infatuated with our meat.

We have a choice: the evil may be patiently borne or savagely resisted.

Dedication

This book is dedicated to the mysterious scrolls discovered in AD 181 inside a tomb at the foot of Janiculum Hill in Rome. History claims that the Roman Senate, led by a praetor named Quintus Petilius, burned the scrolls as a threat to religion.

Table Of Contents

x Mark Mirabello

Preface By
M.L. Mirabello, Ph.D.

'The violation of something private, trembling, and moist arouses them,' whispered a female voice, during an unusual telephone conversation on July 20, 1999. 'With their big, godlike erections, they are rapists by nature.'

Stunned by the unusual declaration—pontificated in a matter-of-fact tone—I said nothing. I simply listened.

'They love to mix blood with their ejaculations,' continued the voice. 'So virgins—untouched by experience—are their preferred victims.'

The woman, who never spoke above a harsh whisper, seemed to have difficulty breathing. After a brief pause, she continued her monologue.

'But their virgin fetish is not indiscriminate,' she whispered. 'They prefer the fresh pudenda of young females—warm and sensual—over the stagnant depths of old maids.'

I was beginning to think I was the victim of a telephone prank—as a university professor, I have been targeted by mischievous students before—but I continued to listen.

Even if the story were a tasteless jest, the stranger possessed a certain lewd eloquence.

'I was only nineteen when they raped me in 1972,' she whispered. 'They stole my pre-sexual innocence—polluted my tender, naked, helpless flesh—and kept me in a cage as a 'breeder.' After years of feeding their ghastly lusts, I managed to escape.'

***

The next day—while I was reading the Kabbala (*Zohar* 3:76)—the peculiar caller suddenly appeared in my office. Clutching a mysterious-looking manuscript in her left hand, she was wearing a Rembrandt-brown cloak.

Brown, I remember thinking, is the favorite color of paranoids. I read that somewhere.

As the stranger stepped into the light, I observed a small woman who was gaunt—even skeletal—in appearance.

She had an unusual face—a face that had been twisted by pain—the pain of someone who had experienced a slow rotting of flesh and soul.

She had queerly pale skin—it looked yellowish-white, as if it had been bleached by some toxic chemical process—and she had strange hieroglyphic symbols branded unto her arms and legs. Curiously, her head and body were completely hairless.

She hesitated—as a hunted wild animal would hesitate—and then slowly entered the office. Her cloak fell open as she walked toward me, and I noticed the clothing of a prostitute.

Specifically, she wore a tight skirt—stained with whiskey, sweat, or semen—and a tattered blouse, yellowed with age. Her small breasts—misshapen and pendulous—were clearly visible through her clothing.

'They actually think humans are ugly,' whispered the woman, who noticed me studying her. 'In particular, they dislike our small heads, our protruding jaws and cheekbones, and our large noses, which appear to be falling into our mouths. Our tiny genitalia—grizzled with hair—are especially revolting to them.'

The woman's septic breath made me wince—it smelled of rotting teeth and bloody phlegm—but I nevertheless offered her a chair.

'Please tell me your story,' I said. 'I want to hear it.'

***

Before uttering another word, the stranger unexpectedly molested my mouth with a fierce kiss. The act was so violent—so savage—I thought she was trying to suck my soul out of my throat.

I instinctively pushed her away and staggered back. The stranger, who seemed indifferent to my reaction, closed the door and seated herself.

'You taste honestly human,' she whispered. 'I had to be certain. The unknown superiors—or their slaves—they are everywhere.'

As the woman and I stared at one another, I noticed her eyes for the first time. They were compelling eyes—clear and green like the eyes of a serpent.

'"The unknown superiors"?' I asked, after a pause. 'Who are the unknown superiors?'

'They keep their existence secret,' she whispered. 'They understand, as Hannah Arendt pointed out, that "real power begins where secrecy begins"—but they are here.'

'And no one else knows about them?' I asked, in a patronizing tone mixed with curiosity.

'A few other humans—certain betrayers of our species— know the facts,' whispered the woman. 'In return for riches and the appearance of power, the traitors—a "fifth column of evil"—guard the doorways to our world.'

'Guard?' I asked. 'Why are guards needed?'

'The monsters fear sunlight,' whispered the woman. 'It makes their skin crack and bleed.'

***

The conversation was decidedly bizarre—even weird—but I decided to continue. Although a historian by training, I have long been intrigued by present-day world views— especially when they are anomalous, apocalyptic, or odd—

and it has always been my opinion that any belief system—no matter how unorthodox—is worthy of study.

After all, when dealing with the human mind, beliefs are more important than facts.

'Tell me,' I said, 'who are the "unknown superiors"?'

The stranger pulled a living insect from her pocket. As it struggled spasmodically in her grip, I noticed it was a sugar ant. Such ants—which have stomachs bloated with a honey-like substance—are considered a delicacy in central Australia.

'Man thinks he is the lord of the organic world,' she whispered, looking down at the ant. 'The top of the food chain.'

'We are,' I declared. '"The most formidable of all beasts of prey," microbes and pests are our only natural enemies.'

'Man is wrong,' whispered the stranger. 'He clings to his fictions—man needs lies like children need toys—but he is wrong.'

'And what is the truth?' I asked. 'Can you reveal it to me?'

The stranger put the insect in her mouth. As she gripped its head with her hand, she bit down on its bloated stomach, crushed the external membrane, and sucked it dry. The taste of the sugar ant, which is supposed to be the sharp sting of formic acid followed the sweetness and fragrance of honey, seemed to give her pleasure.

'There is a higher species,' she whispered. 'A master species—a transhuman species! These creatures—these unknown superiors—they stand above us as we stand above apes.'

'And the master species....' I said. 'Do they live on another planet? There are legends—found among the Dogon tribe in Africa—of a "master species" from the Sirius star system.'

'No,' whispered the woman. 'They are here. Most nest in the darkness beneath our feet—in a complex network of tunnels and caverns that have been slowly—deliberately— carved out of the living rock over the millennia—but some walk among us. In disguise.'

'Disguise?' I asked.

'They have telepathic abilities,' she whispered, 'and they are masters of illusion. Crawling into our minds, they plunder our thoughts and memories, and then, like sinister changelings, they take the places of real humans.'

'A mental patient named Richard Shaver once described similar creatures,' I said. 'And psychologists have something they call Capgras Syndrome, a condition in which someone becomes convinced that a familiar person has been replaced by an identical replica that....'

'It is really happening,' interjected the woman. 'The telepathically generated disguise can be penetrated—the transhuman will appear in his true form, for example, when he sleeps or becomes intoxicated—but the monsters are cautious. The transhuman who replaced a young Austrian named Adolf Hitler—on Christmas Eve in 1906—always slept alone and always avoided alcohol.'

***

The very next day—July 21 to be precise—the mysterious stranger returned to my office for her second and final visit. Still clutching her strange manuscript—and mumbling something about 'the evil down below'—she would make more horrifying revelations.

'The monsters—the unknown superiors—eat only meat,' she whispered. 'Not dead meat—not freshly killed meat—but raw flesh, quivering with life.'

With some hesitation, she handed the manuscript to me. I noticed that her small and grimy hands—which were covered with blue, pink, and green bruises—were clearly trembling.

'I have seen them feed,' she continued. 'Although the transhumans are cannibals—they devour members of their own zoological species—human meat is their staple diet.'

As I looked at the thirty-page manuscript—each page was covered with defaced Christian symbols—my face drained of blood. I actually intuited the presence of ugliness and death.

The cover of the document—fashioned from some kind of blackened leather that was hairy and soft like the skin of a wolf—was emblazoned with an obscene illustration. Painted in lurid colors, the picture had an aura of unspeakable evil.

The illustration clearly depicted a human child—fattened and oiled. The following words, which the biblical Jehovah spoke to man in Eden, were inscribed on the child's body in a bold script: 'you are dust, and to dust you shall return.'

Directly above the child—in an ominous and threatening posture—was a painting of a bloodstained predator clearly identified as a transhuman. The following evil command, which Jehovah god spoke to the devil in *Genesis* 3:14, was inscribed on the transhuman's body: 'dust you shall eat...dust you shall eat all the days of your life.'

'They like the taste of fresh human flesh,' whispered the stranger. 'In particular, they like the soft, white, hairless bodies of young girls.'

***

Working from memory, I have reproduced the particulars of the stranger's manuscript in book form. For emotional effect, I have described her own experiences in the first person singular.

The document itself, which possessed no apparent structure, was a series of notes, declarations, and expressions of terror. Like the Enochian texts of John Dee and Edward Kelly— or the journals of Leonardo da Vinci—most of it was written in 'mirror writing.'

Skeptics will denounce her document as a clever fraud— the product of a scholar, forger, genius—but I make no attempt to evaluate or challenge the woman's claims. In this work, I simply present the fantastic and revolting details.

The substance of her story—that we share the planet with a higher species—a species that can manifest in any form it chooses—has been told by others. John Keel, a noted researcher of the paranormal, calls such entities 'Ultra-terrestrials.' Earlier ages, he claims, called them demons, fairies, or trolls—satyrs, centaurs, or gorgons....

The woman's version, however, is especially powerful. Her 'Unknown Superiors'—her 'transhumans'—breed us like cattle and hunt us like rabbits. With unashamed ruthlessness, they treat humans the way humans treat animals.

Such a story, I believe, deserves to be told.

Chapter I
The Gaunt Stranger's Story: 'How They Raped Me And Ate My Friend Alive'

'I am loath to believe any news that seems probable. Since men are predisposed to believe such news, it is easy to find those who will invent it; whereas the improbable or the unexpected will not be so easily made up.'

Francesco Guicciardini (1483-1540)

'When anyone invokes the Devil with intentional ceremonies the Devil comes, and is seen.'

Eliphas Levi (1810-1875)

Unlike most humans, I would survive my encounter with the master species. Although brutalized by their insatiable sexual perversions, I would somehow endure.

My best friend, however, was not so fortunate. Since she was young and overweight—the kind of fleshy, juicy meat the transhumans relish—she was eaten alive.

Discussing my experience and my friend's death is difficult—
I shudder when I remember the crimes those godlike beasts
inflicted on us—but the facts must be revealed. The truth,
after all, is a laxative for the soul.

Even if it is the unforgettable experience of terror....

Love, Hate, Sorcery

Our horror began—somewhat ironically—on Friday,
October 13, 1972. Still a teenager at the time, I was
spending the night with my best friend, a girl nicknamed
Maddalena. Her home was near Point Pleasant, West
Virginia, a small town on the Ohio River.

Both Maddalena and I were plain, unattractive, and unhappy
girls. Bland and nondescript in appearance—the products
of dysfunctional homes—we were the type that society
cruelly predestines for spinsterhood.

I was small, slim, and angular—with a tiny waist and
featureless chest. Shy and introverted—a bashful virgin—
I always wore my red hair scraped back into a bun. Everyone
said I resembled a thin-lipped librarian.

I never knew my parents—my grandmother raised me—
but I had vague recollections of a perverted old man—
someone who was always drunk and full of lust—and that
man may have been my father. Although grandmother
claimed he never actually molested me, sometimes—during
thunderstorms—he haunted my imagination. I can never
see his face in my mind—that memory has been lost—but

I can remember his awful kisses—and I can remember feeling something cold and flabby against my body.

Maddalena, my dear friend, was somewhat different from me. Overweight and freckled—with large moles on her body—she was vocal and extroverted. A sickly girl who spent a great deal of time in hospitals, as long as I can remember she had suffered from the aggressions of cancer.

Maddalena had more family than I—she was raised by her natural mother—but her home life was not satisfying. Her mother—a practicing nudist who liked to wear only a black girdle and latex thigh boots around the house—was a loud and adulterous woman who had never actually married.

'Fornication is no sin!' her mother used to say, when asked about Maddalena's illegitimate birth. 'Jehovah God impregnated the Virgin Mary, and He didn't marry her.'

***

All the boys in Point Pleasant ignored Maddalena and me— we were 'frigid virgin bitches,' they joked, who were 'saving ourselves for aliens'—but we did not care. We hated boys—mean, cruel, and shallow boys, arrogant with their young, pink, little penises—so we did not care.

Besides, Maddalena and I had each other. Day and night, we were inseparable.

Other girls claimed we were lesbians, and perhaps we were. Maddalena and I were not physically intimate, but I did have fantasies about her. In my dreams I kissed her in a playful and amorous way, and then we made love in the open—in the fresh air—the way wild animals do.

Some would say my feelings were sick, but they were not. My fantasies—although hot with repressed desire—were born of love. They were beautiful, goddesslike, and natural.

You see, Maddalena was special, for with her I felt comfortable. We shared secrets, we dreamed dreams, and, most of all, we read books together. In particular, we studied ancient and obscure works—sinister volumes about legends, sorceries, and beings from other worlds.

We were especially interested in occultism—we poured over stolen texts on Satanism, chaos magick, and the dark litanies of dangerous gods—and in time our interest became an obsession.

Of course, our devotion to the forbidden arts may have been dangerous—H.P. Lovecraft referred to certain 'unnatural pryings into the unthinkable'—but we felt invulnerable.

In our fantasies, we were virgins and witches—the most magickal forms of woman.

Wormwood And Satanism

Around 2:00 AM, not being interested in sleep, Maddalena and I went into the dark forest behind her home to drink absinthe. A green liqueur based on wormwood—the narcotic drug given to the crucified Christ in *Matthew* 27:34—absinthe was our favorite drug.

We knew drugs were wicked and evil—a plunge into horror—but we did not care. Naively believing in the chemical nature of memory and consciousness, we thought taking drugs would expand the radius of our minds.

'Maddalena,' I said, as I poured to the cold earth a libation to demons. 'Let's summon Satan tonight. 'Called "the god of this world" in II *Corinthians* 4:4, he should be accessible to us.'

'An audience with "His Satanic Majesty" would be interesting' declared Maddalena, with a mischievous grin. 'But to invoke the "arch-fiend"—or even one of his angels— we need an aborted human fetus. You know, "a victim too young to scream."'

'But we must try,' I insisted. 'On this night—a night perfect for magick—we must indulge in sin. Beautiful sin, ardent and naked!'

'Well,' said Maddalena, who was an expert on all things occult, 'perhaps we could make a substitution. A severed head—twisted from a living animal—may work instead.'

'Do you really think so?' I asked.

'The "entrails of murdered children" are best,' affirmed Maddalena, 'but we can try.'

***

Maddalena ran back to her bedroom to gather occult paraphernalia for our intended sorcery. As a mistress of the

'Black Arts', Maddalena had purchased and stolen a number of forbidden things over the years.

In a special leather bag—made from the skin of a black cat—she kept her 'weapons of hell.' Items in the bag—most of which were purchased from clandestine sources—included relics from a disturbed grave, dirt swept from a prison, powdered brain from an insane man, dried semen from a corpse (a discharge caused by rigor mortis), a hand-carved crystal (four inches in diameter), a small quantity of asafetida (a substance more popularly known as 'devil's dung'), sodom-apples (an inedible fruit from the desert), and a variety of evil talismans.

In a second bag—this one made from pig leather—she kept her 'poisons of heaven.' Items in this second bag—loot stolen from Roman Catholic and Coptic churches—included three desecrated communion hosts, a degraded crucifix, 'stygian muck' from Ash Wednesday celebrations, the severed foreskin of a dead saint, a 'bell that had been laid nine days on a grave,' holy water polluted with urine, and a large Easter candle carved to resemble a certain tumescent organ.

In a wooden box—made from a real coffin—Maddalena kept her 'literature' or lore. Her collection included a 'book of shadows,' a 'devil's missal,' two occult litanies, a Gascon 'Black Mass of the Holy Spirit' (a blasphemous inversion of a regular mass, it FORCED God to grant one wish), and a dark grimoire called the 'Red Book of Apin.'

In a small casket made of lead (lead cannot be penetrated by good spirits), Maddalena kept special demonic pacts we had drawn up on our eighteenth birthdays. Written with menstrual blood in mirror writing on virgin parchment, in the pacts we renounced the occult junta called the 'holy trinity,' the perverted fable called the 'Bible,' and the stooges the churches called 'saints.'

Finally, in a little cage made from stainless steel, Maddalena brought a black mouse we called Barabbas. Raised from birth by us, Barabbas had been fed a special diet consisting of dog's flesh, unleavened and unsalted black bread, and unfermented grape juice.

Diabolic Preparations

Maddalena and I met in our special location—a deserted goat pasture near a ruined church, a small stream, and dead trees—and we immediately took off all of our clothing.

As every sorcerer knows, nude or 'skyclad' rituals—although magickally hazardous—are more powerful. For that reason, King David of ancient Israel danced naked and unashamed before the so-called 'ark of the covenant.'

'Satan is *salax deus*—the lecherous god,' whispered Maddalena, as she removed her blouse and touched her breasts. 'Hung like a quadruped—hungering for lewd virgins—they say he "fucks like a god." '

'Most males are boring,' I giggled, as I stared at my friend's body with indecent interest, 'but perhaps a well-endowed demon—a lustful incubus from hell—could satisfy even me.'

'I hope so,' whispered Maddalena, half in jest. 'In the shameless invocation we are going to use, you have to chant the heterosexual lines.'

The night air was cold—our young skin was covered with gooseflesh—and as I looked at Maddalena's naked body I had to admire her courage. Even though cancer had eaten away her right breast, she was always a source of courage and joy for me.

'I love you, Maddalena,' I whispered, with lesbian suggestiveness. 'More than life itself, I love you.'.

'And I love you,' she replied, as she softly touched my pale skin and blood-red pubic hair. 'And remember, as long as we have each other, we will always be safe—always be cherished.'

Maddalena removed a stolen communion host from her bag and placed it in her mouth. Although the body of Christ is non-kosher—all animals that are not cloven-hoofed and cud-chewing are non-kosher—we routinely ate such food.

'Kiss me with the host in your mouth,' she said. 'According to legend—a perverse and occult legend—such a kiss keeps lovers eternally faithful.'

'Then we must kiss,' I whispered, as I pressed my little mouth to hers, 'so that we can be forever.'

That special kiss—which tasted like wild fruit—would be our first. Destined also to be our last, it would be a drop of honey in a life of undiluted gall.

***

Holding a consecrated dagger in her left hand—the dagger was a black-handled weapon called an athame—Maddalena cut an equilateral triangle in the damp clay.

'Although addicted to falsehood,' whispered Maddalena, 'Satan must speak the truth when he stands within a triangle.'

Inside the freshly cut figure, we poured a libation of liquor. Made from the blood of the grape, it was red and warm like fire.

'Satan is a flesh eater,' whispered Maddalena. 'Flesh eaters are drawn to alcohol, just as vegetarians are addicted to sugar.'

Outside the triangle, Maddalena sprinkled a small quantity of bluish-green powder. Purchased from a corrupt mortician, the powder supposedly possessed occult power.

'It is grave mold from an old woman who died a virgin,' explained Maddalena. 'Deflowered by maggots—the fauna of death—she gave to vermin what she denied to men.'

Next, we sprinkled some grave dust that my friend claimed had been stolen from the Arlington National Cemetery. The dust—scrapings from a mummified penis—allegedly came from the tomb of a world leader slain in 1963.

'He was a lover of wine, women, and evil,' whispered Maddalena, as she fingered the offering. 'Called "ugly head," he was sacrificed by one whose name means "god's power." ' '

'Some day we must also steal earth from the grave of Lincoln,' I whispered, as I watched my friend. 'A master felon, he caused more American deaths than Hitler, Tojo, and Mussolini combined.'

'But Lincoln freed slaves,' declared Maddalena.

'One person died for every seven freed,' I replied, flaunting my knowledge of history. 'Those are the odds of a psychopath.'

***

We giggled childishly, and then we drew a nine-foot circle of sorcery in a counterclockwise direction on the ground. Inside the circle, we made a pentagram.

'Every eight years,' whispered Maddalena, 'the morning star—symbol of our Lord Lucifer—traces a five-pointed figure in the sky. It is a potent symbol.'

'Jack the Ripper—the left-handed cannibal killer—understood that fact,' I whispered. 'The positions of his murdered victims, if plotted on a map of London, form a huge pentagram.'

Outside the circle, my friend placed a powerful fetish. According to Maddalena, the fetish contained pubic hair stolen from a whore.

'The vaginal pelts of sluts,' she whispered, 'are soiled with lust and crime. Taken from tainted wombs—wombs no man would marry—they are charged with occult power.'

On top of the fetish, we placed an old Bible stabbed by a dagger. Since the Bible is a symbol of violence—there are 375 references to blood in the Old and New Testaments— it is useful in chaos magick.

'Notice the scriptures are open to the Samson story,' whispered Maddalena. 'Samson was the mass murderer who killed over 3000 men, women, and children.'

Next, Maddalena reached into a jar and scooped out some black ashes. She rubbed her eyes with the ashes and instructed me to do the same.

'The ashes are the remains of an incinerated black cat,' she whispered. 'Eyes rubbed with these ashes can see spirits.'

Finally, we lit the desecrated Easter candle and placed it in the circle. According to ancient lore, a candle burns sulfurous blue when a spirit is present.

We Summon The Evil One

Our initial preparations completed, we entered the circle and knelt on the cold earth. Strange thoughts—the raw material of an epic—flooded my mind.

'Now,' declared Maddalena, 'let us begin. And remember, there are two types of magick: that which is futile and that which is dangerous.'

'Do you think we can really summon Satan?' I asked.

'We can try,' replied Maddalena. 'The rite is not always effective—sometimes only lower spirits and pre-human souls appear—but it may just work.'

My friend opened her most potent grimoire—a copy of 'The Red Book of Apin'—and together we chanted sinister incantations. In effect, we pledged allegiance to the forces of darkness.

'Our Father, who wert in heaven,' we murmured, 'hallowed be thy name. Thy kingdom come, thy will be done, on Earth as it is in hell....'

As we prayed, Maddalena removed Barabbas from his cage. I, meanwhile, anointed the nine openings of my body with a special mixture of asafetida and dried corpse sperm. To apply this 'witch's ointment,' I used the middle finger of my left hand.

'O vile Lord,' declared my friend, 'thy name is Satan. Firebrand of freedom—prototype of all rebels—enemy of all totalitarian gods and all authoritarian creeds—we call upon thee this night. Summoned by the blood we shed, hear the magick of the word.'

'Hail Satan!' I intoned, reading my part of the ritual. 'As lord of ecstasy, indulgence, and freedom—as the enemy of toil, abstinence, and conformity—as the foil to the tyrant Jehovah—we call upon thee this night!'

'O Lord Satan,' my friend cried, as she held Barabbas aloft, 'bless our violations. O horned, hairy, and goatlike god—

arcane master of the abyss below—feed us this night with thy power.'

'O rapist god,' I declared, 'come to us. O despoiler of girls—O lustful and proud Lord—we are naked virgins—pure, unexplored forms—and we open for thee. Young, tense, and fragrant—perfumed like fruit—our snow-white thighs ache for thee.

Maddalena stabbed Barabbas with her black-handled athame, and she cut out his eyes, tongue, and heart. Then, she twisted off the animal's head, placed the head in her mouth, and swallowed it whole.

'O horned god,' continued my friend, 'a counter-god who craves blood—not vegetable offerings—come to us. O Prince of Darkness—O Beast of DCLXVI—come to us now. Come now, O outlaw god!'

'Master of lecherous delights,' I shouted, 'we are wet with sin. Come, make us slimy with fornication!'

Something Wicked Comes To Us

After some more chanting—more sacrilege, blasphemy, and crime—something dramatic happened. About 3:30 AM, we heard the falsetto baying of stray dogs, and our candle began to burn with a deep blue flame.

'*Ad Maiorem Satanae Gloriam*,' shouted my friend. 'To the Greater Glory of Satan!'

A cold wind began to blow in from the west. Curiously, the pages of the bible were blown open to *Malachi* 4:6, the curse that ends the Protestant Old Testament.

I looked into the wind, and I saw three lights in the black sky—three globular structures—that were shining and beautiful. The lights, which seemed to be watching us, were accompanied by a scent of plum blossoms. The odor was sweet—almost saccharine—in nature.

'Lord Satan is coming,' whispered my friend. 'Cold and inhuman—"a beauty fresh from hell"—he comes to us.'

The intensity of the lights increased, and I began to feel pain in my head. I tried to cover my eyes with my hands, but the lights were so fierce, so luminous, and so paranormal that I could see them through my hands and closed eyelids.

'*Ad Maiorem Satanae Gloriam*,' shouted Maddalena, this time with some anxiety. 'To the Greater Glory of Satan!'

The lights grew even brighter—still covering my eyes, I could see the actual bones in my hands—and then suddenly there was blackness.

'What is happening?' I whispered. 'What is happening?'

'Lord Satan,' replied my friend, who was now ashen-faced. 'He is here. I sense his evil intelligence.'

We heard a strange sound—a rustling in the weeds—and then we saw a horde of rats, dragging some fantastic and shapeless object across the forest floor.

My friend screamed hysterically and began to run. I grabbed a weapon—Maddalena's ceremonial dagger—and I followed her.

What We Saw

In a clearing, we unexpectedly encountered three human-like entities—a young woman, a younger man, and an elderly woman—floating above the ground, surrounded by auras of greenish light. The entities appeared solid and tri-dimensional.

The younger female was naked except for a loose skirt. Her breasts, which were defined, firm, and magnificent, seemed to leak milk and blood. A rosary—made from small human vertebrae—was suspended from her neck.

The male, who tended to remain somewhat apart, held a twisted cross in his left hand. Naked except for a garish loincloth and a brass nose ring, his penis jutted obscenely through his clothing.

The older female—whose face seemed to radiate contempt—was dressed in a transparent shroud. In her left hand, she was holding some sort of black scroll, an icon of a slain god, and an evil-looking totem.

Directly beneath the three entities, I could see four brownish stains. Oddly, each stain was anthropomorphic in shape.

A diaphanous substance, which resembled silver threads, was strewn everywhere.

The Voices In Our Heads

Although the mouths of the evil-looking entities did not move, we seemed to hear their voices telepathically. I remember noticing that their communications, which had a strange and robotic quality about them, seemed to originate directly inside my head.

The voices, which could be distinguished clearly above a cacophony of other sounds, identified the beings before us as Mary, the Mother of God, Jesus, the son of God, and St. Anne, the mother of Mary and the grandmother of God.

'Salutations,' declared a cold and arrogant female voice. 'Pregnant with revelations, we bring you the Third Fatima Secret.'

'Indeed,' said a coarsely masculine voice. 'The pope, surrounded by his eunuch priests, will never tell.'

'This is the secret....' said a female voice. "*Eloi, Eloi, lama sabachthani*," the anguish of Gethsemane, is the cry of everyman.'

'But since man is not free,' said the male voice, 'man is not guilty.'

'And so,' said a second female voice, 'Armageddon will be a giant party. All the human race—including the dead—are invited.'

Threats And Lies
Although frightened, I pointed the dagger at the entities.

'Stay back!' I shouted. 'I will use this!'

'All women can stab,' said a male voice in my head. 'But not all women can fight.'

'Stay back!' I repeated.

'On your knees,' said a female voice. 'We come from Jehovah—the proud and distant god.'

'Indeed,' said a male voice. 'Your ritual—a magickal provocation—brought us to this place.'

'No!' I declared. 'You must be devils! With a satanic grimoire, we summoned you!'

'I speak the truth,' said a female voice. 'I swear on the skull of God—I swear on the stretch marks of the Virgin Mother—we really do come from Jehovah.'

'Yes,' said a second female voice. 'Do you not know, that blasphemy—cold and pure—is the quickest way to gain God's attention?'

'Exactly,' added a male voice. 'When a wizard called Aleister Crowley baptized a toad, christened it with the name of Jesus, and crucified it with rusty nails, God noticed immediately.

'But Jehovah god—the biblical god—is supposedly an omniscient being who notices everything,' I replied. 'He is allegedly all-knowing.'

'No god is omniscient,' said a female voice. 'That's a lie for children and philosophers.'

'Listen to the truth,' said a second female voice. 'In this reality of ours, gods are simply expert players who move grotesquely carved pieces in a game without rules.'

Utter Terror

There was a moment of silence, and Maddalena, who was terrified, fell to her knees and crossed herself. Moved to piety by the horror, she began to quote scripture.

'If we are out of our minds,' she mumbled from II *Corinthians* 5:13, 'it is for the sake of God....'

I, meanwhile, was transfixed—rooted to the ground with fear—and simply stared at the entities in front of me. Curiously, I kept thinking about the famous Leonardo da Vinci painting, 'Virgin and Child with St. Anne,' and how these entities in no way resembled their Renaissance portraits.

The three creatures before us were, to say the least, strangely odd. Christian entities are supposed to be pure, pristine, sexless intelligences, but these were different. The Mary figure seemed far too sultry—wicked black eyes and sinfully healthy breasts—to be the Virgin Mother. The Jesus figure, who is supposed to be a gelding god—a pale and sterile deity emasculated by guilt and atonement—also seemed inappropriate. Weirdly terrifying—he was covered with deeply cut, snail-shaped scars—the Jesus figure had the eyes of a martyr, the mouth of a lecher, and the hands of a murderer. As for St. Anne, she seemed relatively normal for an old woman—although her dishevelled, iron-gray hair, liver spots, and two or three blackened teeth gave her a haggish appearance—but who ever heard of the 'grandmother' of god?

How The Things Seemed To Change Form

The three figures—still suspended in the air—slowly moved toward us on swirling balls of luminous gas. The method of locomotion was bizarre—even though Jehovah himself, maker of crop circles, allegedly travels in a whirlwind.

As they drew closer and closer, I noticed the strangers seemed to change in size and shape. The transmutation was completed in seconds.

The St. Anne figure changed first. No longer old and withered—she became young, nude, massive, and powerful, with blood-red, needle-pointed nails, fearsome, sharp teeth, and a monstrously obese body.

Moments later, the Virgin Mary figure transformed. Her beauty completely disintegrated within seconds, and she became a nauseating ogress. Shamelessly naked and hideous beyond belief, she now had a pair of great ugly buttocks, a bloody vagina leaking some sort of slimy fluid, and two huge breasts that were pulpy and soft like rotten fruit. Her fearsome breasts—the nipples puckered with lust—moved to and fro like monsters when she breathed.

Finally—and most revolting of all—was the transformation of the counterfeit Christ. Inexplicably, he was also suddenly naked—his loincloth seemed to vaporize before my eyes— and I observed his body change size and shape and color. He became ugly—loathsome—repulsive....

He now had an oversized head with pointed teeth and a large, smooth, hairless body that was yellowish in color. Oddly, he seemed to resemble a monstrous fetus with fangs.

His penis, which initially appeared small, thin, and malnourished, now appeared colossal—gruesomely exaggerated—in size. Throbbing with criminal lechery—sagging under its own enormous weight—it was as long and thick as a small human arm.

Terrifying to behold, it reminded me of a large poisonous snake, a monstrous marine slug, or some freakish leather dildo. Gorged with blood and covered with swollen veins, it emerged menacingly from his groin.

Such an evil thing, I thought, could not please any woman. An abomination, it could only profane and degrade.

A Strange Dream

As the strange beings continued to move closer, I apparently blacked out. Perhaps fear caused me to lose consciousness—perhaps it was the monsters—but I do remember that I had the oddest dream.

I think it was a dream—some sort of vivid nightmare—for I was raped by Satan himself. Using my virgin body—immaculate, unsullied, and pure—his evil plan was to procreate the apocalyptic Beast.

I struggled in the dream against the incubus—I recited the words of *Psalm* 91 which, according to the Jewish *Talmud*, had the power of keeping devils at bay—but the charm had no effect.

'Thou shalt not be afraid for the terror by night; nor for the arrow that flieth by day,' I recited in the dream, with a trembling voice, 'nor for the pestilence that walketh in darkness; nor for the destruction that wasteth at noonday.'

But the devil continued his aggression. Ignoring the psalm of David, he forced his black and chancre-covered penis into the bloody darkness between my legs.

'With my body,' he hissed, 'I thee worship.'

I screamed and writhed—the union of our mismatched genitals was a savage and implacable—and I was delirious with pain and terror.

I begged for mercy, and I shouted the name of Jesus—the love child of Jehovah—but the devil only laughed.

'We will have a baby,' he hissed. 'Between puberty and death—there is birth.'

Worse Than A Nightmare

I awoke from the nightmarish hallucination shrieking. The reality in which I found myself, however, was equally horrifying.

I was lying face down in the dirt—my mouth filled with mud. Oddly, my lips were covered with a black, fungus-like incrustation.

A poisonous foam—some kind of odious-smelling ointment— covered my entire body. The vile substance, which had a harsh, acidic feel, had vaporized all my hair and had given my skin a jaundiced look. The freakish changes, I would later learn, would be permanent.

I struggled to raise myself, but I stumbled. Everywhere, the mud was slippery with blood and vomit, the liquids of death.

I fumbled in the darkness for the dagger—Maddalena's black-handled athame—but I could not find it. The weapon seemed to have disappeared.

'Help us!' I cried, to any power that could hear me. 'Help us! Help us!'

I wanted to run—I wanted to run anywhere—but I could not move. Something was holding me from behind—something with a vice-like grip—something with clawlike hands.

'Help us!' I shrieked. 'Help us!'

I felt spasms of pain in my lower body, and I felt something evil—something utterly obscene—deep inside of me. Immense in size, it seemed to be moving.

The violent intrusion—whatever it was—was caused by something that was hard and cold to the touch. It made me feel unclean—dirty—polluted.

Screaming again, I cried out to my friend. Alone and afraid, I felt small, helpless, and powerless.

The Terrible Crime

I heard a sickening sound off to my right—a sound that resembled the crushing of a crustacean's exoskeleton—and I managed to look in the direction of the noise.

To my horror, something was happening to Maddalena.

I cried out to my friend, but she did not answer. I heard strange communications in my head—moaning, groaning, shrieking and blaspheming in a Babel of languages—but Maddalena was silent. At the time, I assumed she was mute with fear.

I could not see my friend—the two monsters standing over her were blocking my view—but I knew something terrible was occurring.

'Maddalena!' I shouted. 'Maddalena!'

With detached ruthlessness, the monsters with her seemed to be committing an atrocity in a calm and methodical fashion.

I cried out—a wild, maniacal scream—and it was then that I managed to catch a glimpse of my friend's lower body. Her legs—wet with gore—were flailing in some sort of epileptoid seizure. In some areas, the flesh had been pulled completely from the bone.

'Maddalena!' I cried. 'Maddalena!'

Reacting to my shriek, one of the beasts stood erect and looked back at me. It smiled—a twisted, slightly reptilian smirk—and I could see fat, blood, and shards of bone in its teeth. The fragments were unequivocally human.

'Death is inevitable and sometimes abrupt,' hissed a snide voice in my head. 'That is the way of nature.'

What I Saw And Felt Behind Me

Fully expecting to die—thinking I also would be eaten alive—I forced myself to look behind me. Like Orpheus—like Lot's wife—I directed my eyes toward the forbidden.

It was then that I saw another horrible truth.

Sick with desire—aroused by his own raw, elemental sadism—the monster had forced his huge penis into me.

I convulsed with disgust and agony—I could see his icy, tumescent organ glistening with my blood—but my repugnance seemed only to fuel his ecstasy.

His thrusting quickened—his penetration became more furious—and I felt a powerful shudder—an uncontrolled throbbing—deep inside my body.

He made a wicked sound—something between a sigh and a moan—and his face seemed to shiver with pleasure.

The monster grunted—his muscles stiffened—and some kind of sperm—some kind of reproductive filth—jetted from his swollen penis.

The discharge—ejected with great force—was cold and thick and slimy. Resembling congealed pus, it had an offensive, suffocating smell.

'In your womb,' said a voice in my head, 'a meat-eating animal will grow. He will love warm places—but he will hate the light.'

The Monsters Replace Us

'Who are you?' I sobbed, to the monsters. 'What are you?'

'We are three,' said the voices in unison. 'Virgin, warrior, scholar.'

'You are not human!' I cried.

'Then, perhaps we are finite gods,' said a male voice. 'Or, perhaps we are carbon-based demons. Or....'

'Or,' interjected a female voice, 'perhaps we are you....'

I felt a strange sensation inside my brain. It was not a cerebral inflammation, but some sort of telepathic penetration.

'What are you doing?' I cried. 'What are you doing?'

'We are paranormal beings,' said a voice. 'Crawling into your soul, we can brutalize you without even touching you.'

The molestation of a human mind by a transhuman—the criminal trespass on the sacred psychic space called self— is a horrifying experience. Thoughts, memories, desires— everything that is private, secret, and shameful—becomes known to them. A non-genital form of rape, it is the ultimate violation.

'Please stop!' I cried. 'Please stop!'

Nauseated with fear, I felt faint. Even as I swooned, however, I observed that the two female monsters seemed to change size and shape. Oddly, they became replicas of Maddalena and myself.

'Since we are replacing these girls in man's world,' said a voice, 'it is a shame they are not beautiful.'

'Indeed,' said another voice. 'Only pretty girls—the ones with slender bodies heavy with breasts—only pretty girls have any fun.'

I wanted to cry out, but I could not. The scream died stillborn in my throat.

Feeling helpless and violated, I passed out. Only the blackness saved me from madness.

Chapter II
My Years With Things
That Eat Humans

'And the Serpent mounted Eve and injected filth into her; she gave birth to Cain. From thence descended all the wicked generations into the world.'

Kabbala (Zohar 3:76)

'The worms shall feed sweetly on him.'

The Bible (Job 24:20)

Inside The Abyss: What I Found In The World Of The Monsters

For hours—even days—I was unconscious. During that period, my mind was in a bottomless gulf without walls and without light.

When awareness finally returned, I found myself—naked, bruised, and bleeding—in a grave-sized cage made of stainless steel bars. My skin was still covered with dried semen—the spoor of the beast. Remarkably, I was still alive, but I felt bewilderment and fear.

Terrible pain convulsed my body, for both my legs and arms were broken. I would later learn that the fractures—

intentionally inflicted on all abductees—had a purpose. The leg and arm injuries made escape and resistance impossible.

As I looked about, it was dark—although a strange, phosphorescent glow provided some illumination. The air, polluted by the stench of sweat, urine, and chemicals, was hot and stifling. A churning, spiraling fog burned my eyes.

I could see little, but I could determine that my cage was inside some vast interior space—some enormous cavern-like chamber. Water was dripping from the rough-hewn walls, but the landscape of raw rock was devoid of all vegetable growth. Oddly, the place resembled a titanic mausoleum.

I screamed, and suddenly the suffocating air was thick with fiends—vermin startled by the sound of my voice. I saw flying cockroaches, the spawn of some hellish sinkhole, I saw albino spiders, venomous and evil, and I saw enormous black bats, hideous with their shiny, membranous wings. All of these monsters—hissing in a maddening fashion—darted back and forth in the darkness.

The Corpses I Saw From My Cage

From my cage, I could see mutilated body parts—shapeless red heaps—scattered haphazardly on the ground.

Skinned, eviscerated, and split in half—butchered and dismembered like animals—the corpses scarcely looked human.

Adjacent to some grayish bones—bones covered with a strange fungus--I could see a statuesque torso of a black female. Strikingly flawless—with slender, panther-like shoulders, perfect, mahogany-colored skin, and firm, equally splendid breasts—it had neither head nor limbs. I had seen dozens of sculptured torsos in art museums—masterpieces made from imported Italian marble—but now the whole notion of depicting one body part alone seemed revolting.

Some fifty feet from the torso—on the opposite side of the cavern—was the rotting corpse of a pregnant woman. Bloated with foul-smelling gases, her intestines protruded from her vagina and rectum. Between her decomposing thighs—in the cleft between damp hairs—I could see her rotting fetus.

Adjacent to the fetus—near a bloody white bottom—was a severed human head. The head was mangled—the upper jaw and nose were missing, and the skull was fractured on the right side, just above the temple—but the remains of the face gave it the appearance of a young Asian woman. Were she alive, I remember thinking, she would be beautiful.

As I stared at the young woman's dimpled face, it appeared to be moving. Was she smiling in death at me? I wondered. Was she giving me an enchanting, sphinx-like grin?

Then I noticed the reason for movement. The head was an abscess filled pus, stench, and corruption, and it was swarming with fat, loathsome, white maggots. These hellish creatures—squirming as they fed—made the face grimace and move.

I vomited uncontrollably—a watery vomit mixed with slime and blood.

Another Strange Dream: Whores, Priests, And Crucifixions

Heavy with sleep, I slipped again into unconsciousness and had a horrible dream. The dream—the conjunction of the brutal and the fantastic—was based on a blasphemous passage I had read in *Justine*, a pornographic novel written by the Marquis de Sade.

In the dream, I could see two crosses in the middle of a ghastly place—a parched wasteland covered with broken human bones.

Gold, the feces of hell, was scattered everywhere. Swarthy priests—all of them small, ugly, and effeminate—were busily collecting the nuggets. Nearby, a syphilitic old whore—studded with ulcers—was watching them. The whore was laughing.

She must be alive, I thought in the dream. According to legend, dead souls cannot laugh.

Nailed to the crosses were two thieves. Naked except for crowns of thorns, they were called 'Perverted by Wealth' and 'Degraded by Poverty.'

Crucified in an inverted fashion, their protuberant bottoms were visible. In the cleft of the buttocks—in a certain small and obscene orifice—was something that resembled a bleeding heart.

Although most people are dyslexic in nightmares, I could read this inscription on each of the crosses:

'He who died on the cross was only its first victim.'

My Life As A Breeder: How The Monsters Collect Human Wombs—Bloody And Fertile—And Use Them To Produce Food

In the years that followed, I was raped periodically by the monster. Since he seemed to enjoy sexuality at a primitive, blood-soaked level, the rape *always* included violence.

Traumatized by the abuse—fists and feet, teeth and nails were used against me—I came to believe that all sex is pathological.

Ultimately, I realized that we feel our organs—including our sex organs—only when they are sick. Since genital orgasm is the most powerful of all feelings, it must be the greatest of all sicknesses.

***

Since the monsters are extraordinarily fertile—as fertile as cockroaches—I would produce many mutant babies for them.

All my children—the fruit of monstrous crime—the mongrel product of a human eggs biologically polluted by transhuman sperm—were loathsome in appearance.

The least revolting ones had misshapen heads and ice-blue eyes. Soft and fat and evil-looking, they had an extraordinarily thin and translucent skin that was almost transparent. Their shrieks and cries, which were oddly hideous, resembled the squealing of piglets.

Those with birth defects—some had abnormal growths, some were born without anuses or uteruses—were even more horrifying to behold. I still see these mutants in my nightmares.

***

All the babies—whatever their appearance—had short, sad, pathetic lives. Treated like caged zoo animals—faceless homogenous victims—they resembled sinners in the hands of an angry god.

Their existence was meaningless—between the screaming at birth and the howling at death—they knew neither joy nor love. In their lives, there was only pain, grief, and madness.

Some of the babies—the most fortunate ones—were eaten immediately by the monsters. Fresh from the womb—with bacteria-free intestines—they became a sterile and delicious feast.

Some of the babies—the few females who were not infertile hybrids—were designated as future breeders. These were all predestined for rape.

Like their mothers before them, the breeders would know the pain and gore of childbirth. Squatting in their own filth—their distended bellies covered with stretch marks, scars, and stitches—their lives would focus on their wombs.

Most of the babies, however, were fattened for the slaughter. Crowded into undersized cages—deprived of all physical activity—force-fed with milk from brownish, scab-infested teats—they lived two years of misery.

Ultimately they would be seized—beaten to a jelly—and then eaten alive.

The Horror Of Passing Time

Night passed into day, month into year, and I quickly lost all sense of time. In the words of Yukio Mishima, time 'dripped away like blood.'

Treated like an estrogen-injected breeder—a fecund producer of infantile meat for insatiable carnivores—I had to cling to my sanity in this world of menace and terror.

I was normally kept in absolute darkness—an oppressive blackness seems to have a calming effect on caged humans— and I spent most of my time in tormented sleep.

At one time I loved sleep—'when the body sleeps,' declare the legends, 'the soul is awake'—but in the realm of the monsters it was different.

Horrible dreams—lewd and repulsive in nature—constantly afflicted me. Bubbling up from my animal id, I had weirdly erotic visions.

In some nightmares I saw a bloody vagina. Shamelessly exposed—its lips were thick, upturned, and deformed—it was smeared with fresh honey.

Thousands of fruit flies—drawn by the honey—swarmed over the slimy vaginal lips. The tickling of the flies—an unpremeditated act of bestiality—caused frightful and delicious orgasms.

In other nightmares, I had visions of diseased phalluses—ribboned with purple lesions—assaulting me without mercy.

The phalluses were always diminutive in size—as long as a finger and correspondingly thin—but their aggressions were infinite. Erected by my misery, they squirted blood instead of seed.

The dreams were so real—so graphic—that I began to doubt reality itself. What if life itself is a dream—I thought—but we notice the dream only when we are asleep?

Even more horrifying, what if I did not exist? I could be a fantasy—a hideous nightmare—the product of some insane mind.

I cannot remember my birth, so how do I know I was born?

Eating Filth

Trapped in a steel cage, my health deteriorated. Living with death—pelted by the urine, feces, vomit, and other droppings of the babies caged above me—I was plagued by ulcers, pneumonia, septicemia, and diarrhea.

I was given regular doses of loathsome drugs—usually through injection. The drugs were not to make me healthy, but to suppress obvious symptoms and keep me alive as a breeder.

I was also given pesticides to eat. Apparently designed to kill flies and other parasites, the pesticides passed through my body and killed insect larvae hatching in my excreta.

My usual food consisted of putrid rations delivered by a mechanical feeding system. The system, a kind of automated feeding trough, made a hellish sound when operating.

Year after year—feeding after feeding—the food was always the same. A kind of meat paste, it was composed of flesh torn from human corpses.

I initially resisted this horrid diet—I tried to subsist on spiders, lice, and raw worms—but eventually I came to accept the cannibal way. I remembered the words of the Jesus, 'except ye eat the flesh of the son of a man, and drink his blood, ye have no life in you.'

The evil-smelling meat paste, which had a revolting flavor, was always mixed with dried human feces. Since humans, like most animals with one stomach, are inefficient digestive machines—we defecate, for example, about one-fourth of the protein present in rice and potatoes—the dung was fed back to us.

Human farmers are known to inflict the same atrocity on their farm animals. In all worlds, the lower fauna are abused by the higher.

Thoughts On Death
Tormented by life—hounded by suffering—I often thought about death. Called 'the flight of the alone to the Alone' by

Plotinus, death is indiscriminate. 'All beings are destroyed when their time comes,' declares the *Shiva Purana*, 'whether they are gods or mosquitoes.'

Death—inescapable death—is the great mystery. Freud said we cannot imagine our own deaths—whenever we try to do so, we actually survive as 'spectators' watching our own funerals—but still the phenomenon obsessed me.

I knew that approximately 100,000 people perished somewhere on Earth every day, and I wondered what happened to them. What happened after the final breath?

Did the dead evaporate and rise to the heavens—perfect summerlands of light and fragrance—did they descend to a loathsome pit called hell—the eternity of which is stressed in 27 separate Koranic verses—did they return to Earth—reincarnated through the hazards of chance or the so-called 'laws of karma'—or did they join a listless herd of nomadic dead—a horde of unhappy translucent ghosts wandering on the other side?

Or, did the dead simply die? That is what the Bible claims—'The dead know not any thing,' says *Ecclesiastes* 9:5, 'neither have they any more reward.'

In the long run, was man only ozone and fertilizer?

To discover the truth, would I have to 'die and become'?

***

My misfortunes had turned me into a quasi-atheist—if gods exist, I thought, they are too powerless, too indifferent, or too autistic to help us—but I was not prepared to deny the afterlife.

Most atheists, of course, believe there is no post-death existence. If there is no god, they argue, humans simply share the squalid death of animals.

I was certain, however, that the constipated logic of the atheists was flawed. If natural life does not require gods for its existence—if the first organisms, the ancestors of all flora and fauna, emerged spontaneously in the primordial mud—why should afterlife need gods?

Yes, I thought, if life does not require gods for its existence, neither does afterlife. Both are engendered by nature.

Afterlife may not be forever—perhaps a soul lingers only for a time, like the smoke outlasts the fire—but I believed it was a natural process. It was real.

Of course, it may be the exception rather than the rule in nature—like the phenomenon of a mongoloid baby, perhaps afterlife was a rare occurrence—but it still was real.

***

George Gurdjieff taught that survival was the fate of an elite. Ordinary people perish with their bodies, he argued, but extraordinary people lived on after death. Could that be correct?

And if—as Gurdjieff argued—some special people did survive, what made them endure? Was there, I wondered, an elusive boon that bestowed life after death? If so, could it be stolen or purchased like any other treasure?

Or were some souls, I thought, simply stronger than death? If so, what made them stronger?

Human emotion was a potent force in nature—we know that faith can heal and fear can kill—so was passion the answer?

If so, what focused that passion? What invested it with its prowess? Was it the power of virtue? The force of evil? The need—the insatiable craving—to exhaust every variety of pleasure?

What could it be?

Thoughts On Suicide

Trapped in my coffin-sized cage—covered with festering sores—tortured by a monster species—I often thought about death. And—given my predicament—I became infatuated with suicide.

I have never been obsessed with life—life, as one cynic pointed out, is a sexually transmitted disease that always ends in death—so termination was a distinct possibility.

I remembered the command of Nietzsche: 'To die proudly when it is no longer possible to live proudly. Death of ones own free choice, death at the proper time, with a clear head and with joyfulness....' What words of power!

Yes, I thought, glorious self-annihilation is compelling and attractive. Since death is more beautiful than love (the immortal Octave Mirbeau said that), self-destruction would be a brief, almost autoerotic free-fall into a great velvet darkness.

***

Had not the great Yukio Mishima killed himself with a dagger? Thrusting and wet—his hand one with the weapon—Mishima called suicide the 'ultimate masturbation.'

In my night dreams, my suicide was always maternal and affectionate. Nestled like a plump baby in my mother's arms, I parted my lips to suckle a pink nipple rubbed with black poison.

There was a slight acrid taste—a moment of discomfort—and then peace. Smiling sweetly, I rested in bliss.

In my daydreams, my fantasized method of suicide was different. I imagined a radiant death—pure and clean—I died like the incinerated moth that flies into the fire.

How I longed for a dignified end—I could almost smell the funeral pyre of scented wood—but it was not to be.

Although I wanted to die—without fear and without anger—I could not. It was not possible.

My hate—incandescent and pure—kept me alive. And my desire for vengeance—a passion that burns hotter than lust—gave me purpose.

Vengeance gave me the reason to continue.

Chapter III
How I Found Freedom

'It is your duty to learn from the enemy.'
Ovid (43 B.C.-A.D. 17)

My Escape: The Day Of Blood

My escape occurred swiftly and unexpectedly. After years in the hellish, labyrinthian world of the monsters, I found my freedom.

On the day I escaped—the time of blood atonement—I was transfigured.

In my early life, I had always been an anvil. Now, however, I became a hammer.

An Omen Of Doom

My blessed day began inauspiciously. I had a nightmare—a bizarre lucid dream. Curiously, in the dream I could see only when my eyes were closed.

At first I was happy in the dream—I was rich, powerful, and celebrated—I was desired by women and admired by men—but then I looked down and saw a corpse.

The dead body alarmed me. Shaped like a cuddly little pet—a quadruped called 'the Lamb of God'—the body was actually Dogma, the corpse of Truth.

'When the cadaver no longer smells,' hissed a voice, 'the soul is gone.'

Frightened, I tried to flee, but I was stopped by twin sisters. Named Pornography and Blasphemy, they were naked and white, and their mouths were red from feasting on their own children.

'Violence is the key,' hissed the sisters. 'When you are reborn in paradise, all your victims will become your slaves.'

The sisters forced me to eat a certain book—I could not see the title—but it was about the amoral worship of beauty and force. 'Nazism for the Iron Age,' I think they called it.

Devouring the book, which was sweet in my mouth but bitter in my stomach, made me afraid. This was a lucid dream, and I knew that eating books in dreams is an omen of doom.

'I can't die now!' I shouted enigmatically in the dream. 'I want to be the first into the future!'

One More Crime

I awoke suddenly, and I noticed the door of my cage was open. One of the monsters—the same transhuman who had raped me and degraded me and kept me prisoner—was standing over me. In his powerful jaws, some mutilated prey—I think it was a human baby—was writhing in agony.

The little victim reached out to me—strangely, in this hot place, his tiny hands seemed almost blue with cold—but I could not help him.

Before I could act, the monster crushed the baby's head between his teeth—as easily as a man would crush a grape—and sucked out the contents.

The child shrieked—his white bones splintered—and his nose filled with blood.

Averting my eyes from the horror, I saw fragments of a tiny skull—scattered like flowers on the ground.

I was reminded of a sacred cauldron—a holy grail that had been shattered.

Ancient words—harsh incantations from a dead language—spontaneously fell from my lips.

'*Jubela, Jubelo, Jubelum,*' I whispered. 'Head, throat, and heart, I will avenge you, little one.'

Mysterious Words

Casually throwing the remains of his victim aside—only the baby's skeleton and liver remained—the beast seized me with his powerful hands and dragged me from my cage. He was so close I choked on his putrid breath.

As the monster stared into my eyes—a direct gaze that threatened death—he began to utter noise with his mouth. Resembling glossolalian gibberish, I still remember the sounds clearly.

'*Nuk Pu Nuk,*' he said slowly. '*Nuk Pu Nuk.*'

His speech shocked me, for although these monsters are orally fixated creatures who satisfy virtually all their needs via the mouth—they express aggression by biting and pleasure by sucking—they typically communicate telepathically.

'*Nuk Pu Nuk,*' he repeated, this time with greater force.

I have always believed in the power of words—all masters of psychological warfare are skillful verbal terrorists—and I knew the beast was trying to terrify me.

'*Nuk Pu Nuk,*' said the beast. '*Nuk Pu Nuk.*'

Staring back into his eyes, I tried to steel my will. In my mouth, however, I could taste the fear.

The Stigmata Of The Beast

Dragging me some forty yards from the cage, the monster stopped and reached into a satchel of some sort. He extracted an edged device—some kind of technologically advanced branding iron—and he pressed it successively against my cheek, my shoulder, and my thigh.

Each time, the object—which seemed to leak energy—grew white-hot for about three seconds and burned the living skin. Later, when the scabs fell off, I was left with permanent scars.

Then I heard a strange sound in my head, and the monster forced me to the cold dirt. Wallowing in the mud, I felt degraded, humiliated, passive....

I briefly thought again about suicide—whenever I am raped, I think about eating dirt until I die—but the self-destruction fantasy soon passed.

Instinctively, I opened for him. As I had done hundreds—perhaps thousands—of times before, I opened my legs to accommodate the lecherous monster.

This time, however, was different. This time, he no longer seemed interested in traditional vaginal intercourse.

Anxiety overwhelmed me—I feared my blighted womb, ravaged by pregnancy and dried out by time—had lost all value, and I prepared for the worst.

I imagined a red death—a violent death—and I imagined his belly full of my tortured flesh.

A Dream About The Pit And The Worms

Again I blacked out, and I had another vivid dream. It was a revolting nightmare.

In the dream, I was in a rectangular pit—some sort of sinkhole. Covered with filth, I was standing in the black water up to my knees.

'Error is like sin,' hissed a voice in the dream. 'The deeper it is, the less the victim suspects its existence.'

Suddenly, I noticed the earth beneath me was moving. It was not earth at all, but a menacing organic mass—something that was pulsating and alive.

Festering and vile, the slimy mass was made up of thousands of little worms squirming noiselessly in the darkness.

The worms—hideous to behold—resembled small hooded snakes. Ice-cold, flaccid horrors—squirting some sort of poisonous venom—their soft flesh was as white as leprosy.

The albino worms were flesh-eaters—hungry carnivores—and I could feel the gnashing of their sharp, little teeth, as they stripped the tissue from my bones.

I could see dozens of worms twisting and crawling under my skin—the nude skin of my throat and chest—and I was certain I would die.

The victim of silent, swarming invertebrates, in my dream I was certain I would die.

The Taste Of Clammy Flesh

When I awoke from my nightmare—my vivid nightmare—I was on my knees in front of the sexually aroused monster. With lowered eyes, I was forced to perform a lewd act with my mouth.

His phallic aggression was revolting. I choked on his enormous fascist rod—swollen with sin, it seemed longer, thicker, and more terrifying than before—but the brute ignored my emotions.

I wanted to vomit—the thought of his vile penis, only inches from my brain, utterly disgusted me—but I could not.

Gasping for air—gagging on his clammy flesh—I looked up at the beast. I could see his eyes glowing with lust—I could see his thin lips speckled with foam—and I felt rage. Intense pathological rage.

Convulsing with fury, violent fantasies—castration fantasies—raced through my mind. In my imagination, I dreamed of holding his severed penis in my hands.

The monster was now moaning—grunting with animal pleasure—and he seemed too preoccupied to read my thoughts. Instead, his thrusting quickened, and he forced his huge erection—his icy nakedness—deeper and deeper down my throat.

More castration fantasies—more lethal perversions— flooded my mind. Visions of his mutilation—his dismemberment—his vivisection—obsessed me.

The monster began ejaculating—I could taste his grotesque discharge—it was thick, viscous, disgusting—and feelings— ghastly emotions—raced through my heart.

In a few moments, I relived every injury and humiliation that vile thing had ever caused me.

What happened next may sound excessive—even insane— but I will not apologize. Years of torment had incubated my hatred and made it pure.

With manic savagery—like a wild leopard ravenous for meat—I seized his still rigid organ with both hands, and I bit down with the jagged black stubs that used to be my teeth.

It was fine and hot.

* * *

The beast made an inhuman shriek—a demon-like howl—and fell to the mud like a slaughtered calf.

Bleeding and emasculated, he strangely reminded me of a menstruating female. A female with 'the misery and the sickness!'

I pounced on the monster—slashing, gashing, and mauling with my teeth and nails—cursing and blaspheming with my tongue—I instinctively knew what to do.

I wanted to eat him—to make his body disappear into mine—so I gouged out his eyes with my fingers, scooped out part of his brain through the bloody sockets, and thrust the gore into my mouth.

Tasting his brain tissue, which was warm and fresh and wet with slime, filled me with the unashamed will to power.

'The proverb must be true,' I whispered. 'Domination is sweeter than fornication.'

Curiously, the monster's flesh, which tasted like raw fish, vaguely resembled vaginal secretions in odor. Eating the beast—especially the fat behind his eyeballs—therefore had a cunnilingual character.

I tried to eat everything—I wanted to feast until there was nothing left but hard, clean, incorruptible skeleton—but at length I was sated. After devouring the soft flesh of his face and hands—after consuming his spine and testicles—I could eat no more.

I did, however, drink some more of his blood to stiffen my resolve, and I washed my face with the same blood. The crimson fluid—a kind of war paint—glistened in the darkness.

In the life history of any woman, I thought, her holiest moment is when she awakens from her powerlessness.

What I Did With The Castrated Corpse

I wanted to bury the monster face down in a shallow grave—with his mouth filled with dirt and his lips sewn shut—but there was no time.

So I seized the remains of the brute—his dismembered body was still twitching with life—and I dragged him with great effort. As we moved, we left a trail of his blood and fat on the ground.

Eventually—after traveling about 30 yards—I found a womblike ditch—about twenty-five feet deep. Filled with evil-smelling chemicals, the ditch produced great naked flames—over three feet high—and a large pillar of smoke— red like blood. Fortuitously, the bottom of the ditch was studded with sharpened metallic stakes.

Recognizing opportunity—this was my chance to stab him with a metallic penis-substitute—I acted quickly. Spitting into the monster's mouth, I pushed him into the deep, fiery abyss.

My aim was true—the trajectory was immaculate—and I impaled the beast on one of the stakes that protruded up from the flames. With supreme justice, the stake perforated his body through the anus.

Suspended in midair like a butchered animal or a skewered wild pig, the monster died slowly and beautifully.

As I watched his final moments, I compulsively touched myself. I reached down—where it is hard and pink and soft and white—and it was wet with female secretions.

The weight of the monster's corpse, meanwhile, caused it to slide slowly down the stake. Eventually a sharpened metallic tip—glistening with blood and feces—emerged gloriously from his face.

Then—even as I watched—my victim slowly descended into the liquid inferno at the bottom of the ditch.

Dissolving like soft wax—producing a smoky eruption—the body disappeared into a lake of fire.

Fire purifies everything, I thought.

As the red smoke, perfumed with the stench of cremated flesh, drifted up and encircled me, I felt strangely renewed. My youth and beauty were gone, but I had tasted the intoxicating sweetness of vengeance.

Killing the beast, I thought, has restored my virginity and my dignity.

My Flight From The Underworld Of The Monsters

Greased with grime—slippery with blood and sperm—I started my journey for freedom.

I could not move quickly—my right foot, infested with parasites, had long ago rotted before my eyes—but I could move deliberately.

I knew my escape would not be easy—hunted like an animal, I had to flee down nightmare corridors—but I was resolved not to fail.

I had no idea where I was—like the hapless victims in Plato's allegory of the cave, I had no certain knowledge of the reality beyond my immediate surroundings—and the mystery was terrifying.

Was I a prisoner on an alien world? Was I trapped at the Earth's core? Was I buried alive in an unfathomed void of time and space? I did not know, but I did not give up hope.

Somehow, I thought, my courage will take me home.

Crawling In A Tunnel

I found a makeshift weapon—it was the edged device dropped by the beast—and I entered a strange glass-lined tunnel adjacent to the ditch.

I felt like a commando—a guerilla fighter—for I was at war, I was alone, and I was behind enemy lines.

Feeling my way through the darkness, I could sense that the tunnel, which was dark, wet, and cut in a spiral, had a gradual upward slope. The further I advanced, the narrower it became.

Crawling on my hands and knees, I moved as quickly as possible. I tried to concentrate, but random information— thoughts, images, and sounds—all chaotic and horrifying— perforated my mind and filled my head.

When these intrusions are experienced by surface humans, we call it madness. But it is not madness—it is not a schizophrenic episode—it is real. The voices in our heads— the violations of the conscious and unconscious—these are the sounds of the monsters communicating.

'The invaders will not master me,' I muttered. 'To crimes against my mind, I will never submit.'

Horrors In The Suffocating Gloom

After crawling several thousand feet, I felt a wooden door in front of me. I hesitated—I could feel the raw fear at the back of my brain—and I curled up like a fetus.

No, I thought. Purified by years of torment, I have become strong. No longer frail and timorous, I know I can brave the horror.

Focusing my courage, I slowly pushed against the door. Curiously, the old wood crumbled like parched clay—

creating a jagged aperture about three feet across and four feet high.

My heart palpitating, I plunged into the blackness on the other side. The stench was overwhelming—the air was heavy with a graveyard stink—but I did not retreat.

'I must continue,' I muttered. 'I must continue.'

As I crawled on my hands and knees, I could feel the products of fungal growth and decay. Putrefaction—the gradual bacterial dissolution of the body into gases and liquids—had always repulsed me, but I did not give up. Stifling the urge to vomit, I pressed forward.

I seemed to be inside a small shaft of some sort—a crudely chiseled passage or sub-tunnel—and I kept advancing. I encountered something softer than the soil—it was a decomposing body—a corpse swarming with centipedes— and the horror almost made me scream. Fortunately, however, I was able to muffle my shriek with my hands.

The corpse blocked my advance—and I attempted to move the mass of corruption. This was difficult—when I pulled on the arms, they detached from the torso—so I decided to climb over the cadaver instead.

As I crawled over the corpse's head, I noticed that most of the facial features had disintegrated, but its eyes were strangely intact. Covered with blue film—the hideous blue film that covers the eyes of all decomposing humans—they burned themselves into my soul.

When I crawled over the body itself, the cadaver suddenly collapsed. White ribs—jutting from blackened flesh—exuded a peculiar odor. To this day, I am haunted by that sickening smell.

Finally, after some effort, I squeezed by the body and continued my journey. I was encouraged by a glint of light in the tunnel ahead of me.

Eventually, I could feel a second wooden door, and this one I had to pry open with my steel tool. When I at length succeeded, I could hear and feel the hiss of a cold wind.

I peered into the darkness beyond the door. To my utter dismay, the latter tunnel led to the dank cellar of a squalid farmhouse. I recognized the house—located in Parkersburg, West Virginia—it belonged to a fat, quarrelsome, and neurotic old woman who kept to herself and avoided all neighbors.

For years I had been only a few miles from home. The world of the monsters is adjacent to our own!

What I Found In The Old House

I expected trouble from the old woman—she was somehow connected to the monsters—but she was no where to be found.

Indeed, the house was devoid of life. I encountered one diseased cat—my presence in the cellar was a source of terror for him—but I saw nothing else that moved.

With great caution, I slowly walked up some irregular stairs, through the kitchen, and toward the parlor. The house, although filthy and unkept, and littered with excrements in every corner, did not appear extraordinary. I did not observe secret passageways, hidden staircases, fake walls, concealed shafts, or trap doors.

I did notice a cork-lined, shuttered bedroom, however. The writer named Marcel Proust lived in such a bedroom—he slept by day and composed by night—so perhaps he was a transhuman.

The bedroom was dark, but I could discern some detail. In the center of the room—in the midst of peeling wallpaper, falling plaster, an ugly insectivorous plant—I could see occult paraphernalia.

Especially prominent was an obscene illustration with sinister supernatural significance. It was a picture of Death—depicted as a circumcised Asiatic—and he had a colossal night crawler—a kind of repulsive 'conqueror worm'—rising lewdly from his groin. Two kneeling women—both aroused and developed—were greedily kissing the hideous worm.

Directly beneath the illustration, a large triangle was inscribed on an old table. The gutted remains of a neutered puppy—the animal had a plastic bag on its head and a stake through its heart—were positioned inside the triangle.

These words of Georges Bataille were inscribed along the outer edges of the triangle: 'SACREDNESS

MISUNDERSTOOD IS READILY IDENTIFIED
WITH EVIL.'

Occult Pictures And Moldy Books

When I reached the parlor—which was furnished like a
small library—I found another bizarre illustration on the
wall. This one was a crude painting of Adam and Eve—
both dressed in animal skins—and they were fleeing from
the Garden of Eden.

Some overripe fruit—rotten and soft—was crushed under
Eve's foot. Identified as the forbidden food of knowledge,
the fruit bore teeth marks.

'I think I understand,' I muttered. 'Eden was a cage, and
Adam and Eve were pets.'

To the right of the illustration—adjacent to a bell and black
candle—was a cherry wood bookcase. The shelves were
crowded with dozens of moldy books, but one work in
particular caught my attention. Oddly bound, it was a
manuscript entitled 'The Evil Down Below.'

I picked up the manuscript and opened it at random.
Underneath a quotation from the *Gospel of John*—the
mysterious work in which Jesus never tells a parable or
performs an exorcism—were some provocative words:

'Everything known about the master species—their origin,
their culture, their subterranean world, and their hellish
city—is written here. Handwritten in English on parchment

made from human skin, on the 'night of crystal' in 1938. Long live Azazel!'

Azazel—I remember reading in the *Book of Enoch*—was punished for revealing secrets. Intrigued, I decided to steal the book.

A Vision Of Beauty And Ugliness

There was also a basket of dirty clothing on the floor, and I quickly dressed myself. For nearly half my life at that point, I had lived in nakedness.

As I put the clothing on my body, I experienced strange hallucinations. In my mind, I imagined I heard a little girl's voice. The voice was pure, clear, tender.

I turned quickly, and for a moment I thought I saw a bashful child. Dimpled and pink—charming with her faun-like face—she had a pre-pubescent body with small feet.

The child smiled—a quiet and virginal smile—and then she seemed to disappear. In her place, I saw an anorectic teenage girl.

Emaciated and skeletal—thin, sickly, tubercular—the teenage girl had the boyish breasts of an angel. Oddly, her expression seemed both playful and cruel.

'Unlike all wild animals,' whispered the girl, 'human females bleed when deflowered.'

The girl laughed—a strange, sardonic laugh—and then she also seemed to disappear. In her place, I saw the reality of my own reflection in a cracked obsidian mirror.

I had never been a beautiful creature, but now I was forced to see what I had become. Looking back at me in the mirror was the hideous caricature of a human being.

Although under fifty years of age, I was a bald, virtually toothless crone with the hanging dugs of an old woman. Disfigured and mutilated by technology and pregnancy, I had lost my innocence and my youth.

'Did you know,' whispered a voice, 'that the sexual act destroys beauty? A poet said that.'

For a moment—just a moment—I cried.

What I have been, I thought, I can no longer be.

Some Leviathan Metaphors

I felt something hairy, damp, and dirty moving between my legs, and the sensation made me leap with terror. Fortunately, however, it was only the diseased cat of the old woman.

Focusing my resolve, I dried my tears and continued my quest. Moving deliberately toward the front door, my path took me past a weirdly patriotic shrine.

Decorated in red, white, and blue—in occultism, these colors symbolize war, cowardice, and death respectively— the shrine contained three plastic statues. Each statue—

each political icon—depicted an individual American 'founding father.'

I recognized Washington, Franklin, and Hamilton, but they had blood on their hands and homicidal sneers on their faces. Dressed in powdered wigs, makeup, and satin pants, they looked like transvestite devils.

In the service of sinister goals, I thought, the monsters must sabotage our history.

Adjacent to the statues were two black and white photographs. In the photographs, there were thousands of slogan-shouting serfs worshipping two great beasts.

One of the beasts—dedicated to violence and slavery—was emblazoned with a black swastika. Infected with a disease—one that poisoned and starved the mind—he was destined to die young and blind.

The other beast—dedicated to a fat and sleek lie—was emblazoned with thirteen stripes and dozens of pentagrams. Curiously, he was squatting on a mass of clotted filth.

Directly beneath the photographs—resting on an altar-like table covered in hemp cloth—was an antique gun. Covered with cobwebs and unclean fingerprints, it was a nineteenth-century brass derringer.

The weapon of a rebel—the symbols of treason and crime decorated the barrel—the gun was loaded with a diamond-tipped, armor-piercing shell. Stained brownish-red, the bullet was covered with a thin layer of salt.

Curiously, these cryptic words were inscribed on the stock of the weapon: 'When Dirt And Scabs Are Washed Away, Sometimes This Causes Blood.'

I took the weapon and the ammunition.

What I Found In The Sun

I opened the front door with some difficulty—turning the corroded brass handle required both hands—and I walked outside. Initially, I was overwhelmed by the blaze of daylight and fresh air—I felt pain in my eyes and lungs—and I was reminded of the trauma a baby must experience when she first enters the world. In spite of the pain, however, I was free.

Never again, I thought, will I be enclosed or dominated.

It was early morning, and the sunrise, which was blood-red, was an omen. I thought about the crimes of violence that had liberated me, and I remembered the words of Krishna in the *Bhagavad Gita*: 'all undertakings are surrounded by evil, as fire is surrounded by smoke.'

As I looked at the sunrise, I noticed some green shoots arising from dead and decomposing vegetation at my feet. It was then that I understood a great mystery.

New life, I thought, emerges from death. And to increase life, we must increase death.

I reached down and picked some wild flowers. Since flowers are the genitals of plants, they have always fascinated me.

These are the symbols of love, I thought. When I was a child, my heart once opened like a flower.

I thought about Maddalena and I was sad. Without her, I knew I would always be alone.

Killing Innocence

Turning on to gravel path—a path that bisected a plot of poisonous weeds—I walked over to a small pond.

A young swan—graceful and white—was cavorting in the water. Her life, I thought, was a comedy of innocence.

I seized the swan with both hands. As the animal struggled vainly in my firm embrace, I felt like a masterful lover.

In Buddhism, I thought, to eat an animal is not a crime. The sin is with the killer.

I smiled—my first smile in years—and I twisted off the swan's head with my bare hands. A disciplined act of ferocity, I showed no cruelty.

As I tasted the blood-stained meat—still warm with life— I remembered more ancient words.

According to the Hindu *Vedas*, I thought, everything is food for what is higher.

After eating my victim—I lingered over the fleshy parts— I knelt down to wash my face in the pond. As I saw my own reflection—this time in the sunlight—a horrible realization filled my mind.

My destiny is to be a fugitive, I thought. Fantastically changed by my experiences, I can never rejoin the human race.

'People would not understand,' I whispered. 'Doubting my story, they will put me in a madhouse or a circus.'

Another Strange Dream: Death, Sperm, And Gods

Exhausted by my experiences, I must have blacked out. Once again, I had the oddest of dreams. It was both beautiful and terrifying.

In the dream, I awakened to find myself in northern Egypt. I was in a fabled city, the place where the head of the great Osiris was buried.

'Hail Osiris!' shouted a voice. 'Thou art older, better, truer!'

The dismembered bodies of Palestinian gods—their faces frozen in the dry orgasm of death—were scattered everywhere. Obviously the victims of violence—the gods had been stabbed, strangled, burned—the remains were already beginning to decompose in the desert sun.

Two dogs, the symbols of loyalty, were guarding the divine cadavers. Meanwhile, flesh flies were busily laying their eggs in noses, mouths, and ears of the corpses. Already, some of the eggs had produced maggots.

I diverted my eyes from the scene of death—far from the city—and I saw the plushly female breasts of Mother

Nature. Young and fresh and beautiful beyond imagination, around her there were no plants without flowers or trees without fruit.

Amun-Ra—the creator god of the Egyptians—was standing above the open thighs of Mother Nature. Muscular and bronzed—with beautiful tattoos on his sunburnt flesh—Amun-Ra had a great phallus which stretched across the void of space.

With North African lewdness, Amun-Ra began to masturbate. A peevish god named Iavoth wanted to stop him—in magic, Iavoth was the demon of spurious guilt—but Iavoth failed in his efforts. Sterile and anaemic, Iavoth was too weak and too dead to prevail.

Now I understand, I thought in the dream. In the dead soil of my soul, I understood the truth.

Rubbing his blood-swollen organ—shamelessly seething with life—Amun-Ra ejaculated into the darkness. His vehement discharge—his eruption of white and sticky sperm—squirted against the black skin of the sky goddess.

The origin of all things, the semen of god became the Milky Way.

Chapter IV
The Question Of
Madness

'Every thought, however swiftly suppressed, has its effect on the mind.'

Aleister Crowley (1875-1947)

'In short, the nature of the hallucinations of Jesus, as they are described in the orthodox Gospels, permits us to conclude that the founder of the Christian religion was afflicted with religious paranoia.'

Charles Binet-Sangle (1868-1941)

My Time In A Homeless Shelter

When I eventually regained consciousness, I found myself in some sort of 'Homeless Shelter.' Thankfully, I remained in the human world.

Dressed in cotton pajamas—sitting in a red arm-chair—I still possessed the manuscript, but my weapon was gone.

If the monsters find me here, I thought, I will fight. I will use fists, feet, and teeth.

Exhausted, I tried to fall back into sleep, but it was impossible. The smell of sickness—the stench of sweat and medicine— kept me awake.

My Contact With Insane People

Vagrants and human oddities—the excrements of society— were everywhere in the shelter. Judging from their inexplicable outbursts, most of them were obviously and utterly insane.

An effeminate boy—a strange creature with a male physique and female body language—was a special nuisance. Claiming he was the reincarnation of Pope Julius III—a homosexual pope—the boy kept touching himself in a quasi-masturbatory fashion.

'Behold the miracle!' he exclaimed, as he indecently exposed himself. 'Hardened by desire, behold the resurrection of the flesh!'

Next to him was a fresh-faced girl named Lyssa. She claimed to be a rape victim, but I noticed evidence of masturbation on her pajama bottoms.

'Seduction is worse than rape,' Lyssa mumbled over and over again. 'Seduction corrupts the mind—rape merely pollutes the body....'

On the far side of the room was an old man who believed he was a prophet. A religious fanatic—he had not washed since his baptism—the old man claimed that self-induced head injuries gave him mystical experiences.

'Jesus—the Judaic avatar—is coming back,' he declared. 'After killing all the sinners in an apocalyptic "final solution," he will herd the faithful into a totalitarian paradise. His reign—a kind of "Christian Reich"—will last one thousand years.'

The old man laughed—he was clearly looking forward to eschatological collapse—and then he slammed his head against the floor.

'Heaven will be perfect bliss,' he continued. 'A splendid utopia, it will be a place without crime and without choices.'

What The Psychiatrist Said To Me

An arrogant man—apparently some sort of mental health worker—took an interest in me. An ugly individual—he was short, squat, and blond—he had flaccid lips and rotting teeth.

'You were mumbling in your sleep last night,' said the ugly man, as he placed his hand on my shoulder in a patronizing fashion. 'You said something about "the master species."'

I hesitated to speak with the ugly man—I could see the denial, ridicule, and scorn in his smile—so I stared at the floor.

Silence is best, I thought. This man could be a beast in disguise, so I will act deranged, catatonic, and mute.

'You may suffer from Munchausen Syndrome,' said the ugly man, who ignored my effort to ignore him. 'That's a compulsion to make false reports about personal victimization.'

I must say nothing, I thought. He is obviously a psychiatrist—psychiatrists are immune to logic—so I must show no sign of recognition, warmth, or self-pity.

'Or,' said the ugly man, 'perhaps you are having a paranoid delusion. You are really convinced that subterranean predators—creatures infesting hidden tunnels—are attacking us from the bowels of the Earth.'

Silence, I thought. Oblivious to the world, I must stare with vacant eyes.

The ugly man smiled. His wrinkled face was twisted with sarcasm.

'Don't worry,' he whispered. 'In the safety of this place, you will heal. Here, no one is sickened by freedom.'

Thoughts About Reality

That night, while resting on a flea-infested bed at the shelter, I thought about everything the ugly man had said.

Initially I thought he was a fool—a smug idiot. His mind, I thought, was rusted shut by prejudice.

It was raining outside, and the roar of thunder filled the room. Outside, sinister flashes of lightning blazed across the horizon.

But could I be delusional? I thought. Could it all have been a dream? To babies, the dream state and the waking state are equally real. Could I have confused nightmare with reality?

Lightning struck a tree outside. The tree, which fell with a great thud, began to smolder and burn.

No, I thought, if a thing causes pain, it is real.

I stood up and walked over to a window. In my reflection in the glass, I could see the blood clots in my sunken eyes.

We are what we remember, I thought. Memory is all that matters.

The lightning flashed again, illuminating the room. In the brief moment of brightness, I imagined I could see my father. Standing near a stagnant pool of whitish liquid, he was leering at me.

Yes, I thought. Memory is all that matters. We must not escape from history....

Chapter V
Reading The Mysterious Manuscript from the Old Woman's Home, I Learn About The Origin of the Monsters

'Man has no body distinct from his soul; for that called body is a portion of soul discerned by the five senses....'

William Blake (1757-1827)

'The gods eat other gods.'

Maori Chief (19th century)

The Secrets Of The Book

While staying in the asylum, I studied the mysterious manuscript I had stolen from the house.

Later—in my own handwriting—I would add a description of my experiences with the beasts.

Writing, I quickly discovered, helped me exorcise the horror.

Facts About The Master Species

The transhumans are descended from one ancient matriarch who incestuously mated with her son. Since they derive from a common mother, they refer to themselves as 'the chosen family.'

In the present era, about 22 million transhumans infest the tunnels beneath our feet. We outnumber them—like the fish of the sea outnumber the men with the hooks—but the transhumans are the stronger species.

With their supernormal endowments—their telepathic abilities, vast intelligence, and enormous strength—the monsters can molest our minds, neutralize our science, and destroy our bodies.

The transhumans—the master species—are the focus of all evil.

How Transhumans And Humans Are Related

According to true science, transhumans and humans are related. Long before the beginning of remembered history, we had a common ancestor.

This common ancestor, an imbecilic and filthy primate who walked erect, was a degraded herbivore. Foraging in large groups—innocuous, vegetarian herds—he peaceably ate fruit and grain and acorns.

Cerebrally primitive—simple and bovine—he even lacked consciousness. He had no awareness of awareness.

For thousands and thousands of years—a huge and tedious slice of history—this inoffensive, self-satisfied creature stagnated.

Surviving on instinct, he was a beast among beasts....

***

Then, around the time the Earth lost its second moon, the HUNGER came. Perhaps it was caused by drought—perhaps it was caused by ice and cold—but the plants died, and our ancestors starved.

Hunger produced aggression, and hunger changed our peaceful forefathers. They became carnivores—hunters and drovers who fed on animal flesh. Raw, living animal flesh.

The ancestors discovered the pleasure—the almost orgasmic joy—of eating meat. They felt intoxication when their teeth entered the flesh of their prey—they felt ecstasy when they smelled the blood, tasted the warm fat, and heard the groans of their victims.

But still the hunger continued. The famine was merciless, and there were not enough animals to feed the hunters.

Ravaged by starvation—maddened with hunger—the ancestors began to stalk one another. They became cannibals. They began to defile their mouths with the meat and blood of their brothers.

The ancestors became enslaved to the practice—the thrill of violation is addictive—and their appetite became insatiable.

In particular, the ancestors developed a taste for brain tissue. Extracted from freshly crushed skulls, they found the pinkish-gray tissue soft, moist, and delicious.

The last development—feasting on living brain—was especially important, for food is the engine that moves evolution. Not the struggle to survive—not Darwinian waste and bloodshed—but diet causes evolution.

Since the essence of a living thing resides in its tissues, we become what we eat.

How Omophagia—How Cannibalism— Changed The Ancestors

Omophagia—the horrid act of eating living flesh—is the key to primate advancement.

It is the supreme irony—that crime causes progress—but it is also fact. We cannot deny the fascism of nature.

But how can such a thing be possible?

Unknown to human science—ignorant human science— living flesh is the most potent of all foods.

When an eater consumes such flesh—raw, bloody, and alive—he absorbs and assimilates into himself the qualities of his victim.

Thus, sucking the blood of youth—drawn from the slender arms of a healthy, cheerful, and beautiful girl—is a method of rejuvenation.

Feasting on fresh ejaculate—licked from a withered sexual organ—is a source of passion and desire.

Eating a mouthful of living muscle—bitten from a brave warrior's chest—conveys courage and power.

And, most importantly, by devouring ripe brain—the fabled food of knowledge—eaters assimilate the germs of intelligence.

Rich in the essence of soul—the concentration is especially marked immediately beneath the skull, just behind the forehead—brain is the food that made the development of memory, imagination, and reason possible.

Fresh brain—raw and bloody and alive—is the ambrosia of gods.

Transfigured By Cannibalism, The Ancestors Develop Intelligence

Thousands of years passed, and the savage cannibals gradually evolved. The act of filling their bellies with living, tortured primate flesh—the act of feasting on souls—slowly elevated our ancestors above other animals.

The evolution was gradual—the effects of devouring the soft, wet contents of any cranium are minute during one life span—but in time the results were dramatic.

Over the millennia, the prehuman beasts became manlike. And—ultimately—these manlike creatures began to reason, to imagine, and to speak.

'Man came into being through cannibalism,' wrote an intuitive German named Oscar Kiss Maerth. 'Intelligence can be eaten.'

The Fire From The Sky: How Man Became What He Is

Then, around 30,000 years ago, a FIRE FROM THE SKY ravaged the Earth. This catastrophe—a lethal and beautiful event—changed history forever.

Perhaps a huge meteoroid caused the fire—perhaps a nearby star exploded—but a great wall of liquid flame devastated the planet.

Virtually nothing was safe from the FIRE FROM THE SKY. It incinerated forests, boiled tropical seas, and melted polar ice caps.

Where the meat-eating primates managed to survive, they were usually disfigured. Seared by the holocaust, their burned faces had hollow sockets, and fluid from their melted eyes ran down their blackened cheeks.

Injured, blinded, and traumatized, they staggered across the scorched surface of the Earth. Bewildered and afraid, they encountered a landscape covered with burnt organic remains.

To stay alive in the ruins of a broken world, the meat-eating primates learned to eat the charred remains of the dead. Learning to eat such food was not easy—the fat was yellow and the flesh was dark—and cooked skin tastes like animal scabs—but the desperate can always conquer disgust.

Indeed, goaded by necessity, eventually the meat-eating primates became accustomed to the diet. In time, they even learned to take pleasure in dead tissue.

These polluted scavengers—these eaters of burned, broiled, and boiled cadaver meat—are the direct ancestors of modern man.

Because we eat dead meat—a soulless animal act—we are what we are.

It is the fiat of nature....

The Origin Of The Master Species: The Story Of Korah, The Mother Of The Monsters

When the FIRE FROM THE SKY devastated the planet, one meat-eating primate completely escaped the horror. Called Korah by the master species, all transhumans trace their descent from this female.

She is the matriarch—the mother of the brood—and they are the 'chosen family.'

(This Korah—in a completely garbled form—appears in the Bible. In the sixteenth chapter of '*The Book Commonly*

Called Numbers,' she becomes a 'man' who was swallowed by the Earth for resisting Moses.)

The escape of Korah was quite by accident. A young and pregnant female living in the Zagros Mountains of the area now called Iran, Korah was looking for a place to give birth when she encountered two copulating snakes near a natural cleft in the rock. Intrigued by the omen, she entered the crevice and discovered the opening to a huge interior world.

Stumbling about in the darkness—fingering the cold and slimy rock—Korah found a colossal gallery hollowed out by nature. Since the crust of the Earth is naturally vesicular—filled with cavities—caves and tunnels exist in abundance.

Squatting in the blackness—terrified and alone inside the womb of the Earth—Korah gave birth to twins. She bore two sons.

She called them 'Life' and 'Desire for Life.'

After washing her babies in the cold water of the cave, Korah returned to the surface world, but the world she had left was gone.

Since the fiery holocaust had occurred during her labor, she could not find the bright skies, fresh air, singing birds, and rustling leaves she had left. She saw only blackness, smoke, and ashes.

***

Frightened by her experience, Korah retreated back into the cave. In that rupture in nature, she found a refuge.

Since the FIRE FROM THE SKY had destroyed everything she had loved, she resolved to become a creature of darkness. Filled with supernatural dread, she would henceforth hate the sun.

Calling upon ancient gods, she made this solemn vow: 'In the dead of night—before the white frost of morning appears on the land—I will hunt. And like the fox—but unlike the wolf—I will conceal myself in order to attack.'

Since any new creation—including the birth of a new way of life—requires ritual slaughter—Korah consecrated her oath with blood.

She selected her smaller child—an undersized boy with a puny and insignificant penis—and she ate him alive.

In a cave—a hideous mineral landscape—her victim's final shrieks echoed.

***

In the years that followed, Korah would mate with her surviving son. Because of this union—a primal act of archaic incest—she would become the mother of a powerful race.

Over the millennia, this race—Korah's descendants—would become more than human. Ripening in the darkness—feasting on living flesh—they developed godlike brains and satyr-like loins.

Today, on the evolutionary scale, the transhuman stands supreme. William Shakespeare called man the 'paragon of animals'—but Shakespeare was wrong.

Chapter VI
The Nature of
The Beasts

'And the woman said unto Saul, I saw gods ascending out of the earth.'

Bible (1 Samuel 28:13)

'In her abnormalities nature reveals her secrets.'
Johann Wolfgang von Goethe (1749-1832)

The General Shape Of The Monsters

A transhuman is roughly hominid in shape. When encountered in their true form, they appear to be hairless humans with enlarged heads and hypertrophied sexual organs.

Their bald heads are bulbous, with a large protuberance to accommodate a massive brain. They have small noses, small ears, and small mouths equipped with thin lips and small, pointed teeth. Their almond-shaped eyes, which have the oriental epicanthic fold, appear large and soulful and are perversely enchanting. Their eyes, which are sensitive to light, are entirely pink, without irises or pupils.

Their hands and feet appear human—except the nails—if such talons can be called nails—are long and hard. Like wolves, they typically walk on the tips of their feet.

The skin, the largest of their sense organs, is yellowish in color, like the wax of an old candle. Completely hairless, it is hypersensitive to ultraviolet radiation, and a few hours in sunlight makes it crack and bleed. Wrinkled from birth, their skin hangs loosely on their bodies.

Curiously, the transhumans seem to have insufficient sweat glands. Thus, although they breath oxygen, they prefer to stay around or in water in warm weather. That is why most contacts with these creatures will occur in association with water: fresh rainfall, springs, lakes, or rivers.

Gender Differences

The bodies of the males are arrogantly robust. Lean and deadly, with defined, firm, herculean physiques, the transhuman males are about six and a half feet tall and weigh about 250 pounds. Their massive torsos—which lack the vestigial nipples found on human males—are muscular and taut.

The bodies of the females—if such caricatures of the feminine form can be called female—are smaller and stouter and uglier. Aesthetic atrocities, the females are about six feet tall and weigh about 350 pounds. Menacingly overripe, they have pot bellies, well-fed thighs and buttocks, and huge breasts studded with brown-colored nipples.

For their size, both male and female transhumans are remarkably powerful. A transhuman adult can easily crush human bones without using tools.

Sex Organs

Among primate species, meat eaters have the largest sexual organs. As the most carnivorous of primates, the transhumans have the largest genitalia.

(Flaunting their sexuality, these shameless creatures rarely wear clothing. Although fond of jewelry—such as copper bracelets, silver anklets, and bronze nose rings—they believe clothing is the ceremonial regalia of savages.)

The transhuman penis, an evil abnormality, is gruesomely exaggerated in size. When awakened by lust, it resembles a long and thick boa snake.

Their testicles—each the size of a small orange—possess extraordinary fertility. Whereas the typical human male will ejaculate only 18 quarts of semen in his lifetime, a transhuman male, with his spectacular orgasms and seemingly inexhaustible virility, will discharge about up to one-half cup of reproductive fluids per sexual release.

To accommodate the reproductive protuberance of the males, the females have big and greedy vulvas. Indeed, the female genitalia—gaping chasms that are foul and enormous—are so large that painful childbirth is unknown among them.

The labial lips of the females—red and moist like poisonous spring flowers—hang from their groins like slabs of meat. The clitoris—a monstrous deformity—has the length and girth of a small human penis.

According to the superstitions of these monsters, females are actually the equivalent of castrated males. The vagina, which they believe is a flesh wound—a gaping wound that bleeds—is a supernatural injury. The female is cut by nature to create 'a magic door' so that souls may enter this world.

As long as the vaginal injury is fresh—fertile because it is bloody—the female can bring forth children. When the wound heals—when menopause occurs—the female becomes sterile.

Life is by wetness, say the transhumans, and death is by dryness.

Double Brains:

The transhumans have two brains: a primary brain inside their distended skulls and a secondary brain located in the abdominal region.

Their binary brain system allows them to project and receive thoughts beyond their bodies. Unlike humans, their highly evolved minds are not limited by the sizes of their skins.

The radius of their minds, however, is not infinite. The strongest ones—especially developed adult males—can project and receive thoughts up to a 1000 yards away, but the exercise of telepathy at such extreme distances fatigues them.

Telepathy And Its Uses

The monsters use telepathy as their primary method of communication. Only lower animals, they believe, communicate with sounds or gestures.

The monsters also use telepathy—which they call primary intellection—to help them hunt. Utilizing their double brains as a weapon, they confuse and stampede their prey with telepathic assaults.

The telepathic prowess of these monsters—although formidable—can be defeated. Although they can influence their victims—causing hallucinations, planting suggestions, creating false memories—they cannot compel.

A strong human will can neutralize their cerebral aggressions. In the battlefield of the mind, the human can triumph.

Hallucination And Its Uses

The telepathically induced hallucinations of the monsters— 'tactical lies,' as they call them—are especially dangerous.

During their stealthy forays into our world, these masters of illusion can appear in any number of forms. Always seen at night, they may appear as puritanic gods, bringing commandments or revelations, beautiful succubi, flaunting their high and youthful breasts, androgynous angels, pulsating with light and fire, ghoulish old vampires, lusting for blood and shapely flesh, kindly space travelers, conveying messages of hope and peace, and malignant grey aliens, stalking victims for their vivisections.

Most terrifying of all, the transhumans can even make themselves invisible. Often mistaken for ghosts or poltergeists when they are in this form, the transhumans can telepathically suppress the sensory areas of the human brain and literally disappear from sight. The targeted victim—an unfortunate man, woman, or child--is then eaten alive, raped, or abducted by unseen horrors.

Feeding Habits

Technically, the monsters are omni-carnivores. Since 'the blood is the life,' they will eat anything that lives and bleeds.

The brain—a special repository of spiritual power—the seat of memory, judgement and thought—is their favorite food. When pinkish-gray in color, it is considered especially delicious.

The liver—which they consider poisonous—is always extracted and discarded.

When eating humans, the monsters classify their victims as giants, dwarfs, and worms. These correspond to adults, children, and embryos respectively.

Although dead flesh is normally tabu to these creatures—eating carrion, they believe, shortens the life span—there is one exception. In a special religious ritual, they will eat animals (including humans) killed by lightning.

During all feedings, they allow no metals to touch their food. Believing that metal poisons meat, they eat with naked hands.

Cannibalism:

True to their fiercely predatory nature, these monsters love to devour one another. Although the supply is finite, they believe transhuman meat is the most perfect of all foods.

When one transhuman eats another, however, the indulgence is always surrounded by taboos. Called a 'Cannibal Hunt'— the time when 'souls are torn with violence from beautiful flesh'—the practice is restricted to special times in special places with special methods.

Only lower animals—such as humans—are eaten without ritual.

'Thrill Killings'—A Crime In The Eyes Of The Monsters

All 'thrill killings'—all simple murders in which no flesh is eaten—are strictly prohibited by transhuman law and custom.

Killing without eating—something that occurs in human wars—is a crime against nature. No predator, say the monsters, should ever squander death.

According to their ancient superstitions, uneaten murder victims return as vengeful ghosts. This applies to all species.

Chapter VII
The Life Cycle Of The
Master Species

'The grain produces the seed, and the seed produces the grain. Learn from this.'

Occult Teaching on the 'Circle of Life'

The Infancy Years Of The Transhumans

After the copulation of these monsters, baby transhumans are born after a long pregnancy. Typically, the child spends eleven months in the maternal darkness of the womb.

There are always two babies—always identical twins—per pregnancy. The infants, who are normally delivered about ten minutes apart, typically laugh at birth. The crying of newborns is a characteristic of only lower or 'simian man.'

Most transhuman babies are born healthy, but the few who are sickly, puny, misshapen, or obviously imbecilic are devoured immediately by the parents. Strict eugenicists who have evolved beyond compassion, the transhumans believe that inferior offspring—the so-called 'useless eaters'—should not be allowed to pollute the species.

The healthy newborns are welcomed into the world with an ancient ceremony. Anointed with a mixture of fresh blood and fresh earth, they are given 'names of power' by the mother. The father, meanwhile, devours the afterbirths and umbilical cords.

Transhuman babies usually learn to walk within hours of leaving the womb. (Like the legendary goddess Athena, these creatures really have no childhood.) Highly precocious, no transhuman ever has to crawl.

Feeding The Monster Babies

Transhuman babies feed on milk until the age of six months. They are violent eaters—aggressive obscenities who often bruise and injure the teats of their mothers.

At six months, the twins are given their first taste of blood. Called the 'Blood Sacrament,' the mother tears off a primate head and holds it aloft so that warm arterial fluid runs down on to her bosom. Her hungry babies—cowering in the shadows of her colossal breasts—are forced to lick the blood from her nipples.

'Milk is for infants,' she declares, as she watches her twins feed on the crimson fluid. 'Blood is for adults.'

What Happens When The Monsters Grow Teeth

The twins live on blood until they grow teeth. Most transhumans have a full set of teeth by the age of one year.

Once they have teeth, the children can then eat raw meat and brain. In another venerable rite, the 'Sacrament of the

First Flesh,' the child is given his first meat with these words: 'This victim dies so that you may live. In all future time, do this in remembrance of him.'

The whole ceremony is carried out with great solemnity. Their 'first kill,' like our 'first love,' is a life-shaping experience. The first time in anything, they believe, has a kind of magical efficacy.

The victim for the 'sacrament of the first flesh' is carefully selected. He must be strong, healthy, and unblemished, and must belong to the master species. As the highest of all organisms, transhumans make the best of all possible food.

To guarantee that the first meat is perfect, it is the custom of the transhumans to feed one of the twins to the other. The smaller or less energetic sibling is eaten by the stronger.

In this first meal—a grisly ritual death—no food is wasted. The sibling chosen to survive is first starved for a few days (to insure he eats with enthusiasm and desire), and then he is fed his brother piece by piece, starting with the extremities.

To keep the meat alive and fresh, the victim is slowly dismembered over several days. Non-fatal mutilations come first—all critical organs are kept intact and alive as long as possible—but ultimately the dying twin is tortured to death. In effect, he dies 'a death from a thousand cuts.'

This evil feast—the supreme outrage of fratricidal cannibalism, of sibling devouring sibling—helps a transhuman child to grow up intelligent, strong, tenacious, and purposeful.

Later Childhood Of The Monsters

A transhuman child has the intelligence and strength of a human ('simian man') adult by the age of four. Although they are still considered children by their own species, they are old enough to hunt humans in our surface world.

After making a pact with a sanguinary god named Az, the neophyte joins his first predatory band. Like wolves, the transhumans form aggressive hunting packs.

From the older hunters, the novice learns his craft. After mastering the technique of moving by night and attacking by surprise, the novice learns the locations of the exits to man's world, the typography of the 'killing fields,' and the peculiar vulnerabilities of the human race.

Early in his education, the novice is also taught how to identify the distinctive scent of preferred victims. The sense of smell—the most emotive of all senses—is hypersensitive in transhumans, and at a great distance—with their nostrils quivering like those of hounds sniffing their prey—they can detect the fresh scent peculiar to healthy, lesion-free humans.

The adults also teach the neophytes the art of culling the human herd. Strays—individuals travelling in isolated districts at night—are the most convenient victims, but any large gathering of people—soldiers in battle, devotees at prayer, spectators at concerts or sporting events—are opportunities for feeding. When thousands of human strangers mass together, they never seem to notice the disappearance of four or five people at the edges.

Puberty

At the age nine years, the transhuman enters puberty. From that age, they have a 'duty to breed.'

Although these perverse beings are pansexuals—they will mate with any species and any gender—their first sexual encounter is always a frightful orgy with their own fathers. The incest taboo, which is common among lower animals, is unknown among these monsters.

The first sexual experience of the transhumans—the 'Rite of the White Stains'—is the moral equivalent of rape. The transhuman male—incapable of tenderness or affection—bites, penetrates, thrusts, and pollutes. A tyrant during copulation, his penis is a living weapon.

When the transhuman father rapes—when he ejaculates his reproductive filth—his preferred orifices are the mouth and the vagina. The anus, the sewer of the body, is viewed with contempt. Only a lower primate—such as simian man—would use such a vile playground.

Adulthood

At roughly the age of thirty, the transhuman becomes an adult. Swearing an ancient oath—the 'Oath of the Four Obligations'—the beast promises to 'rule, fight, hunt, and procreate.'

When the female monsters come of age, they celebrate a sickening rite which involves food, eroticism, and torture. The males, in contrast, signify adulthood by circumcising themselves with their own teeth.

During the male circumcision ritual—a ceremony characterized by perversion and degradation—the excised foreskin is proudly eaten by the father of the monster. The mother, meanwhile, sucks on the wound until the bleeding stops.

All adults—males and females—are allowed to participate in the 'Cannibal Hunts' against their own species. Held in the tunnels thirteen times a year—always during the time of the dark moon—the Cannibal Hunts are the most sacred events in the life cycle of these monsters.

During the Cannibal Hunts, small warrior bands stalk one another. Similar to the 'Flower Wars' of the Aztecs, the purpose is to provide victims for a gruesome feast.

Suicide: How The Beasts Become Gods

The ancient Mayans of Mesoamerica believed suicides, who had their own protective goddess, would enjoy bliss everlasting.

The transhumans have a similar notion. Those able to commit suicide, they believe, become the blessed dead—the powerful dead.

By killing themselves, these monsters believe, they can 'make death die.' Willful self-destruction, they believe, is always followed by reincarnation in higher form.

Transfigured, they will return as gods.

How The Monsters Eat Themselves Alive

To become gods—'hunters on the other side'—the monsters practice a special suicide ritual. Called a 'celibate death,' they must eat themselves alive.

To perform the deadly sacrament, the monster returns to the place of his birth. According to custom, his remains must be buried in the exact spot where he was born.

After rubbing his body with honey, milk, and salt, the transhuman climbs into a freshly excavated pit. There—in a pre-meditated act of self-destruction—he will slowly starve himself to death.

This death fast—the so-called celibate death—is a method of autocannibalism—eating oneself. Deprived of food—growing thinner and thinner—the body literally begins to digest itself.

'May my flesh melt from my bones,' declares the transhuman as he begins his terminal fast, 'like the sap that drips from a burning tree.'

Starving to death—which normally requires forty days and forty nights—is a hideous process. As surplus fat disappears, the skin becomes darker, drier, and more wrinkled. Females miss menstrual periods and become sterile—males become impotent. Gradually, the pulse rate and respiration slow, and the victim feels constant thirst, general weakness, and coldness in extremities.

Finally, ravaged by hunger, the neck cannot support the weight of the head. By this time, the emaciated victim is too feeble to walk away from his own wastes.

In the end, he suffers convulsions, paralysis, and death. According to their traditions, he will be re-incarnated as a god.

How To Destroy A Transhuman

For all of their power, the monsters can be defeated. Since they bleed, they can be killed.

With an edged weapon, the best method is to stab the brain, the eyes, the genitalia, or the area between the chest and the belly.

The eyes, which expose the soul, are especially vulnerable. Attacks to this region are usually lethal.

When slaying the beasts—as when causing any violent premature death—always remember to taste their flesh before they die.

Chapter VIII
The Evil Empire: The Tunnel World Of The Master Species

'Great holes secretly are digged where Earth's pores ought to suffice, and things have learnt to walk that ought to crawl.'
H.P. Lovecraft (1890-1937)

'It is not on any map; true places never are.'
Herman Melville (1819-1891)

'One has to visualize a vast underground terminal city, being a branch of a subterranean, suboceanic network of tunnels....Most of these ancient tunnels are now covered at their openings....'
Robert Ernst Dickoff (1951)

'Those who dwell there are possessed of great powers and have knowledge of all the world's affairs. They can travel from one place to another by passageways which are as old as the kingdom itself.'
Louis Jacolliot (1837-1890)

'We were always there, only you have not noticed us.'
Quoted to Carl Gustav Jung (1875-1961)

The Tunnel World In Human Legend

In garbled form, every human culture has legends about a subterranean world. Read between the lies, and there are truths in myths.

Thus, Irish legend describes the mysterious domain of the Formorians—underground carnivores who demand two-thirds of the human children born each year.

In North America, aboriginal myths talk of the hideous realm of the 'Moon-Eyed' people—evil troglodytes who shun the light of the sun.

And in Asia, ancient Indian texts describe monstrous beings that could assume illusionary forms. Called the Raksasas, they have huge stature, great strength, and frightening features.

The Hidden Gateways

Throughout humanity's world, the tunnels have their openings. Some gates are in the wilderness, some are in small towns, and some are in the middle of large cities.

They are always camouflaged and concealed—detecting them is difficult—but the gates are here.

Especially significant openings are near the ruins of an abbey, in Kilwinning, Scotland; inside an occult bookshop, near the British Museum in London, England; under a medieval cathedral in Chartres, France; under Vatican City, a triangular section of Rome, Italy; under a private library, in the ancient town of Bovino, Italy; along the Weser River, near Hamelin, Germany; somewhere in the Pripet Marshes in the Ukraine; by the Black Temple, near Benares in India; under the Potala Palace, in Lhasa, Tibet; adjacent to Uluru (Ayer's Rock), in Australia; in the Yucca Mountains, 100 miles northwest of Las Vegas, Nevada; under Archuleta Peak, near Dulce, New Mexico; adjacent to an old graveyard in Atchison, Kansas; near the Greenbriar Hotel in White Sulphur Springs, West Virginia ; under Mount Weather, near Bluemont, Virginia; in an old house in Port-au-Prince, Haiti; somewhere in a wealthy suburb of Buenos Aires, Argentina; along the Orinoco River, in Venezuela; on the legendary Isle of Demons, in the Atlantic Ocean; close to a hospital, in Kano, Nigeria; and in the city of Mombasa, on the Indian Ocean in Kenya. There is an especially infamous portal somewhere in the Drakensburg Mountains in South Africa.

The Human Traitors Who Guard Gateways

In man's world, the tunnel openings are always guarded by human underlings. These criminal gatekeepers— treacherous humans who serve the monsters in exchange for money, power, and life—are called 'insiders.'

At any given time across the globe, there are about 300 insiders. Abject slaves, they honor and obey the monsters.

Lethal devices—implanted in the heads of the insiders— insure their loyalty. No larger than the head of a pin, a simple telepathic command causes a reaction with the surrounding tissue. Within moments, the victim's brain blackens and dies.

With special effort, the insiders can be recognized. The monsters give them a drug—a white and creamy substance—and this drug strangely pollutes their breath.

To recognize a gatekeeper, remember this sign: their saliva will be the liquid of a wet nightmare.

The Subterranean World

Extending for thousands of miles—illuminated artificially with luminous gas and strange phosphorescent lights—the vast underground dominion of the monsters is a masterpiece of diabolic engineering.

Although naturally occurring tunnels form the core of the network, most of the labyrinth was manufactured by the master species.

Using a ground disintegration technique, the monsters have earth-boring machines which travel on crawler treads and produce white-hot jets of flame.

Such machines, which melt their way through solid rock, excavate cleanly. Vitrifying as they go, they leave a neat, glass-lined tunnel behind them.

The tunnels, which extend into every continent, were seen and described in the twentieth century by Richard Shaver:

> *I repeat, with the most positive finality, the caverns do exist, and they are incredibly extensive... The caves are connected by broad highways, carved through solid rock for thousands of miles, the whole inner Earth being a vastly complicate network of tunnels....*

The Nameless City, The Place Sometimes Called Dis

There is one significant city in the subterranean dominion of the transhumans. This accursed metropolis—infamous for cruelty and excess—is the center of their depraved civilization. Frightening and ugly, the city is a soulless sprawl made up of stone and steel and grime.

The nameless place is sometimes called Dis. Remembered as Asat in Hindu lore—fabled Asat, the dwelling place of demons —Dis is located in an enormous funnel-shaped cave somewhere under Eurasia.

Ancient beyond imagination, Dis is cut right into the crust of the Earth. Insects and rodents and fungi are the predominant wildlife—pollution, toxic waste, and the other sludge of their civilization bubble up and form cesspools throughout the settlement. A black river—oily with petroleum—bisects the settlement.

Along the city's twisted and irregular streets, colossal structures—whitewashed with lime and always cubical or pyramidical in shape—loom in the darkness. Huge oblong monoliths—obscene phallic totems covered with grotesque carvings—break the monotony.

Hell would be a city much like Dis.

The King Of Dis

The city of Dis is ruled by a king. Living in seclusion and luxury, the king is a despot who rules by decree.

In a civilization where murder and rape are honored—in a culture where prestige rests on violence and sexual activity—the king is the most evil member of an evil species.

Bearing the honorary title of 'He-of-a-Thousand-Testicles,' the king is a symbol of power. He carries a rod of iron—from this rod comes flashes of lightning and rumblings of thunder—and any transhuman encountering him must perform the three KISSES OF SHAME. The kisses are applied to the king's naval, his penis, and his anus.

The king sits on an ancient emerald-colored throne. Around the throne are four automated machines, and they are covered with artificial eyes, in front and in back. In perpetuity, the machines play the words: 'Holy, holy, holy is the Lord almighty, who was, and is, and is to come.'

Inexplicably, the king mimics the tyrant described in the fourth chapter of the *Book of Revelation*.

The Sacred Precinct: Shrines To Demon Gods

At the center of the city—adjacent to the emerald throne—is a monstrous temple complex. Constructed from enormous slabs of basalt, the temples are covered with sheets of skin flayed from human souls.

Here the Order of the Trapezoid—an archaic conclave of priests—commit nameless crimes in honor of sadist gods. Oddly obsessed with their religion—a cult of violation and fetishism that includes bloody sacrificial rites—the transhumans believe that any contact with a god has 'magickal' benefit—even if the contact is hate.

***

The temples in Dis belong to the most fearsome gods. Since benevolent deities harm no one—such gods are charming and innocuous—they are ignored.

Carved from the living rock, the largest temple by far is dedicated to the Lord of Death. A wicked idol—forged from meteoric iron—depicts the Lord of Death as a monstrous being covered all over with gaping, foul-smelling mouths.

A supernatural predator who feeds on the souls of the recently dead, this brutish god is 'He-Who-Causes-Death-In-The-Afterlife.' Alluded to in our Bible, the feast of the Lord of Death is called 'the supper of the great God' in the *Book of Revelation*.

According to legend, the Lord of Death ensnares his victims like a spider god. Although hideously ugly, he disguises himself as a loving, open-armed figure—a god, an angel, or a nurturing mother—floating in a tunnel of light. Unwary souls, duped by the enchanting illusion, come too close and are immediately devoured. Expecting beatification, they experience destruction.

In the next world—as in this world—beauty and danger, seduction and torment, are indissolubly conjoined.

***

The second largest temple in Dis is dedicated to a repugnant deity called the Worm God or Serpent God. A despot of great power, to see him is to become blind, to hear him is to become deaf, and to touch him is to die a horrible death.

The worm god is so frightful—in demeanor and appearance—that no one dares to make images or idols of him. He is the 'God-Who-Must-Not-Be-Pictured.'

Inside his temple, next to masculine icon—an enormous brazen pillar that is hundreds of feet high—an oblong box made from wood and gold rests on a tripod. The box, which has a removable lid, is filled with divine spoor. Euphemistically called 'manna that fell from heaven,' the spoor is really droppings from the rectum of the Worm God.

(The spoor in the box, according to the legends, signifies this great mystery: gods are the excrement of nature; nature is the excrement of gods.)

The Worm God appears in human history. The Bible describes how 'Moses made a serpent of brass, and put it upon a pole' (see *Numbers* 21:9), but a reformer named King Hezekiah was opposed to the cult, and the king 'broke in pieces the brazen snake Moses had made: for unto those days the Children of Israel did burn incense to it.' (see 2 *Kings* 18:4).

In Japan, the worm god appears as Amanjaka—the tapeworm deity.

****

The third largest temple is dedicated to Baphomet, the head-hunting god. Baphomet's idol—which is normally covered by a leather mask made from human skin—is a crudely carved crystal skull. Unspeakably ugly, the crystal skull is viewed in a blasphemous ceremony that is performed only once a year.

Utterly insane—a victim of incurable madness—Baphomet suffers from multiple personality disorder. A trinitarian monster, he is one god with three distinct personalities.

Although he is capricious and unpredictable, Baphomet is usually a sanguinary deity, and anyone approaching this god's temple must sprinkle blood from his own body. Those who refuse, it is said, experience death or madness within one solar year.

On a daily basis, the priests of Baphomet offer this dark god the heads of the 'virgins of the sun.' Taken from pre-pubescent girls and boys abducted from the surface world, the heads are always ripped from blameless children who are sweet with virtue. All the victims—all the designated expendables—have hair of gold.

In the grisly ceremony—a dark ritual called the 'Oracle of the Flame'—the priests throw the heads into a hungry black fire. According to their lore, they can predict the future from the shape of the flames.

In human history, Baphomet's most famous disciple was named Salome. Celebrated for her voluptuous beauty—'a beauty which had the right to be cruel'—she gave her god the head of John the Baptist.

The Human Slave Market

East of the temple complex is the human slave market. Since the transhuman species despises work—these indolent monsters sweat only when they play—all physical toil is performed by human slaves.

Most slaves sold in Dis are abducted from the surface world, but some are especially bred and raised for labor in special livestock farms.

Whatever their origin, all slaves are given surgically administered brain lesions. They are lobotomized to make them docile and obedient.

Female slaves are also given special tattoos on their left arms and foreheads before they are sold. Male slaves are neutered.

The castration of the male slaves is especially cruel. With adults abducted from the surface world, the scrotum is cut open without anesthetics and the testes are cut out or pulled off. (Common complications are hemorrhage, gangrene, and maggot infestations.) With males born into slavery, a common method of nonsurgical castration is to place a tourniquet around the newborn's scrotum just above the testicles. Without a supply of blood, the testes become numb in about an hour. Eventually, they will atrophy, decay, and fall off.

Human Meat Market

Adjacent to the slave market is an enormous meat market. Since one living human yields only 18 pounds of quality flesh—enough to feed one transhuman for one week—the market is vast in size. Here, the monsters can be seen walking by cages and picking human victims the way we pick live lobsters.

At the center of the meat market, free-ranging humans are sold. These are men, women, and children ensnared from the surface world during transhuman 'hunting and gathering expeditions.' Producing a fine and succulent meat—one that is sweeter than pork—the best parts are the brains, hearts, thighs, and arms above the elbows.

On the outer edges of the meat market, farm-bred humans are sold. (Transhumans learned to domesticate humans about twenty-eight thousand years ago—approximately the time that humans learned to domesticate the dog.) Raised in cages—fattened on a special diet of bananas— these domesticated humans go to their deaths with the innocence of grazing cattle. Their unsightly meat, which bleeds imperfectly, is considered inferior in quality.

Scattered here and there throughout the market, special kiosks retail frozen human heads. The transhumans have mastered the art and science of cryonic suspension—they can freeze all or part of a living being and reanimate it centuries later—and they use the technology to keep severed human heads alive in specially insulated jars. Although transhumans prefer fresh meat, they will eat reanimated frozen flesh when necessary.

There are rumors of a more hellish commerce—a black market which sells the meat of resurrected humans—dead humans brought back to life—but this, however, is illegal. Although all transhumans know how to reanimate cadavers—for these creatures, reviving even a rotting corpse is a simple exercise—the action is absolutely tabu.

According to their ancient law code—the so-called Brazen Tablets—any transhuman who resurrects the dead will be executed.

Loaded with chains, the condemned monster is alternately immersed in vats of boiling and freezing water until his skin falls from his body.

The torture completed, he is finally eaten alive.

The Arena: Lethal And Perverse Games

West of the temple complex—near the main gate to the city—is a vast public arena. Designed for entertainment, in the arena the transhumans indulge their craving for sadistic amusements.

All recreational whippings are held here, as are the gladiatorial-like contests where humans fight to the death. In the latter, men unusually fight men, but sometimes dwarfs fight women, hunchbacks fight cripples, and blind men fight children.

The fights in the arena are savage and merciless. All the human combatants are naked and weaponless, and before the fight-to-the-death begins all contestants must shout: 'Hail to the Master Species. We who are about to die salute you!'

Before the violence, the spectators indulge their evil voyeuristic fantasies. Obscene performances—utterly lewd in nature—are conducted without shame or scruple.

In one vile spectacle, terrified humans are sexually abused with the dismembered parts of dead animals. Inexplicably, the monsters find this amusing.

In another spectacle, fascinated transhumans watch as fat green worms—loathsome penis substitutes—are forced head-first into the vaginas of human women. As the worms struggle to free themselves—squirming voluptuously and spasmodically—the terrified females scream with revulsion and shudder with pleasure.

In still another spectacle, transhumans roar with laughter as certain human males—selected because they have taut little penises—are raped by transhuman females.

The experience is obscene—given the low body temperature of the transhumans, penetrating the icy coldness of their grave-like wombs is a quasi-necrophilic experience—and the sexual congress always culminates in violence. The transhuman female—like an amoral black widow spider—covers her terrified consort with 'kisses that bruise.' Ultimately, she will devour her consort's head.

When devouring the head, the sport is to leave the brain stem intact. With half a brain, the male's pelvic thrustings continue even in death.

The Nests Of The Monsters

South of the temple complex—extending deep into the groin of the Earth—is the residential section of Dis.

Excavated from the rock, the residential section is composed of hundreds of thousands of cubicles. Shaped like a vast insect nest—a strange hive-like structure—the monsters are crowded together like wasps or ants.

As a rule, each housing cubicle accommodates one family. Although strangely dysfunctional—the typical family is composed of perverted males and degraded females—it is nevertheless cohesive.

Since monogamy is unknown among them (no primates higher than gibbons are really monogamous), a transhuman family can be quite large. Traditionally, it is composed of one adult male and his harem of sexual slaves.

Oddly, for all of their violence, the transhumans are social animals. Fiercely independent, they are afraid of being alone.

A Center For Depraved Science

On the north side of the city is a research facility and science complex. This is the brain—the nerve center—of their paranoid and advanced civilization.

Devoted to wicked science—the hostile domination of nature—the complex is composed of thousands of gloomy laboratories. Here, legions of amoral researchers—greedy for knowledge— commit crimes against bodies and ideas.

***

The most infamous part of the complex is the 'Life Science Unit.' In this nightmarish unit, caged, mutilated, and traumatized humans are subjected to genetic manipulations.

Skillful bioengineers, the transhumans have produced dozens of mutant strains of the human species. The mutants, who are scarcely anthropoidal in shape, are used as livestock, slave labor, or as a source of raw materials.

Some of the mutants are especially revolting to behold. These include the dairy women—human females genetically engineered to produce copious quantities of cream and milk. These females, whose do nothing in life except eat, sleep, lactate, urinate, and defecate, have grotesquely large breasts—glandular atrocities that are covered with varicose veins and up to six or more nipples. Weakened by genetic engineering, poor diet, lack of exercise, and the disadvantages of life in a cage, the dairy women are too weak to support the weight of their colossal mammary glands, and they usually move about on their hands and knees, dragging their inflamed nipples on the ground.

Equally monstrous are the worker humans. Designer-made slaves that are engineered for a lifetime of docile, servile labor, the worker humans are mutants with steroid-injected, muscular, full-sized bodies and small, grapefruit-sized microcephalic heads. They possess great strength and stamina, but their retarded minds are incapable of language or conscious thought.

Most revolting of all, however, are the pig humans. Artificially fattened through genetic engineering, growth hormone injections, force-feeding, and a lifetime of mandatory inactivity, these obscenely obese creatures may weigh over 1600 pounds. Scarcely human in appearance—their faces are masses of flaccid flesh that wobble in every direction—these shapeless monsters are considered unfit for eating, but their large skins are used to make leather and parchment, and their huge fat deposits are used to make soap, lubricants, and salves.

Manufacturing Horrors

Adjacent to the science complex—near a huge salt lake traversed by steel bridges—is the industrial district of Dis. Inside hellish factories—geometrically shaped buildings that are several square miles in size—lobotomized and castrated human slaves produce a variety of manufactured goods.

The soulless factories resemble huge Stalinist work camps. Thousands of workers—swarming like rodents—perform their labor in a mindless and methodical way.

Of all the industrial plants, the most infamous is the soap factory. Here, human fats and oils are heated with potash to produce a soft, dark, harsh, and evil-smelling soap. The work is carefully supervised—adding too much fat to the product produces a soap that turns rancid in days, and mixing too much potash produces a soap that can peel skin from the body—and incompetent workers themselves become ingredients in the vats.

In all the factories, conditions for the workers are horrific. Confined to small cubicles and chained to their machinery, the factory slaves live a life without sunshine, fresh air, or freedom. They are deliberately malnourished and routinely brutalized.

All factory slaves suffer from symptoms which resemble radiation sickness. Exposed to toxic waste and noxious chemicals—often moving cauldrons of poison with the gangrenous chunks of dead, blackened flesh that used to be their fingers—the slaves suffer from fatigue, nausea, vomiting, loss of teeth and hair, decrease in red and white blood cells, and internal bleeding.

The factory slaves work until they are too injured, too weak, too old, or too deranged to continue.

Then, their tumors and malignant sores are cut off and devoured. (Because cancer tissue is ageless, ingesting tumors has a rejuvenating effect.) Finally, the exhausted and mutilated slaves are eaten alive.

Epilogue:

'I am a living animal, tied to a dying soul.'
Philip Dick (1928-1982)

'Men will go about like swine eating the acorns found amidst the putrefaction of their dead.'
Giovanni Battista Vico (1668-1674)

'Evil is older and will prevail.'
Occult Proverb

My Flight From The Homeless Shelter

Holding my precious manuscript, I stealthily left the homeless shelter. Exiting from a window, I fled in the dead of night.

As I dropped to the wet earth, I saw a dog vomiting dirt and grass. The dog—a lean and filthy creature—began to growl.

I picked up a large stick and threw it at the mongrel. Like any dog, he reacted by biting the stick that hit him, not the person that threw it.

Humans are like dogs, I thought. They never attack the real source of their misery.

My Life As A Fugitive

My destiny is bleak. I am indifferent to death—I have no dread of hell and no expectation of paradise—but I do fear the monsters. Every night—I know—may be my last.

For the moment I am free, but I can no longer live a normal life. A homeless nomad, manoeuvering between death and madness, I can never rest in peace.

Since the monsters track, ambush, and ensnare by night, I move only by day. To cover my scent, I usually travel only when it rains.

Solitary and aggressive—a fugitive in my own world—I live like a scorpion. Trusting no one, I abide in constant fear. Paranoia, as they say, is heightened awareness.

To support myself—to pay for food, clothing, and shelter—I have become a prostitute, the second oldest profession. Covering my deformities with a long cloak, I am a fellatrice. That is to say, I am paid to perform oral sex on repulsive and perverted old men.

I hate those old men—filthy beasts with their pubic scabs—wasted by desires they need whores to satisfy—but they give me an opportunity to feed.

Thanks to my profession, I can indulge in the most basic of cannibalistic acts: the swallowing of semen during fellatio. Fornicating with my mouth, I eat the life of the men I hate.

Prostitution carries risks—disfiguring gonorrhea, maddening syphilis, and cancerous A.I.D.S. are constant threats—but I do what I must do.

Postscript
By M. L. Mirabello, Ph.D.

'Be ye therefore wise as snakes....'
Jesus of Nazareth (Matthew 10:16)

Last Words With The Mysterious Stranger

When I had finished reading the manuscript, I looked up at the woman. She was feeding on another sugar ant.

'Ingestion is the ultimate act of domination,' she whispered. 'The victim is absorbed by the eater—body and soul are absorbed—and all that remains is excrement.'

I nodded my head in agreement, and the woman smiled. Then, she reached into her pocket, retrieved still another sugar ant, and gave it to me to eat.

'You must torture it first,' she whispered, with perverse logic. 'Terror-stricken animals taste better.'

I placed the beast in my mouth. I could feel it squirming on my tongue, and the experience was not pleasant.

'Savor the moment,' whispered the stranger. 'A first kill—like a first love—is a special experience.'

Acting almost instinctively, I swallowed the helpless creature. A faint feeling of nausea touched me.

'Violating the animal, you have completed the sacrament,' whispered the woman. 'Your victim is now bound consubstantially with your soul.'

The Odin Brotherhood by Mark Mirabello

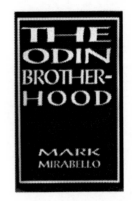

ISBN 1869928717
£9.99/$20 in paper

'When the world is pregnant with lies, a secret long hidden will be revealed.' - An Odinist Prophecy

Just like the *Cannibal Within,* a chance encounter, although this time in the famous Atlantis bookshop, blossomed into a dialogue between the author and the anonymous adept of Odin. Called an "occult religion" for adepts, a "creed of iron" for warriors, and a "secret society" for higher men and women who value "knowledge, freedom and power," the Odin Brotherhood honors the gods and goddesses of the Norse pantheon.

This non-fiction book details the legends, the rituals, and the mysteries of an ancient and enigmatic movement.

**For this and details of other Mandrake titles contact: Mogg Morgan, (01865) 243671
email mandrake@mandrake.uk.net
web: mandrake.uk.net
PO Box 250, Oxford, OX1 1AP (UK)**

Lightning Source UK Ltd.
Milton Keynes UK
16 February 2011

167630UK00001B/14/A